The Advocate's Memory

Teresa Burrell

This book is a work of fiction. References to real people, events, establishments, organizations, or locales are intended only to provide a sense of authenticity and are used fictitiously. All other characters, and all incidents and dialogue are drawn from the author's imagination and are not to be construed as real.

Cover Art by Madeline Settle

Edited by LJ Sellers

Library of Congress Number: 2022911725

ISBN: 978-1-938680-35-9

Silent Thunder Publishing

San Diego

Dedication

This book is dedicated to the hundreds of thousands of people who suffer from myalgic encephalomyelitis, otherwise known as chronic fatigue syndrome. An estimated 836,000 to 2.5 million Americans suffer from ME/CFS, many of who go undiagnosed, and as a result untreated.

Also, to those who suffer with memory loss, or have a loved one who has gone through Alzheimer's or some form of dementia. These are horrible, debilitating diseases that affect not only the patient but their loved ones as well.

Acknowledgements

I want to thank the following people for their continued input and help as I continue down this journey:

Tara O'Neil CHt

Jennifer Ross

Alex Velasquez

JP

Thanks, **Elona Thomas,** for choosing the title for my book.

And My Loyal Beta Readers:

Beth Agejew

Linda Athridge-Langille

Vickie Barrier

Denise Bowman

Melanie Cardullo

Teresa Harden

Alisha Henri

Crystal Kamada

Sheila Krueger

Janie Livingston

Joy Lorton

MaryAnn Schaefer

Colleen Scott

Uma Van Roosenbeek

Denise Zendel

Also by Teresa Burrell

THE ADVOCATE SERIES

THE ADVOCATE (Book 1)
THE ADVOCATE'S BETRAYAL (Book 2)
THE ADVOCATE'S CONVICTION (Book 3)
THE ADVOCATE'S DILEMMA (Book 4)
THE ADVOCATE'S EX PARTE (Book5)
THE ADVOCATE'S FELONY (Book 6)
THE ADVOCATE'S GEOCACHE (Book 7)
THE ADVOCATE'S HOMICIDES (Book 8)
THE ADVOCATE'S ILLUSION (Book 9)
THE ADVOCATE'S JUSTICE (Book 10)
THE ADVOCATE'S KILLER (Book 11)
THE ADVOCATE'S LABYRINTH (Book 12)
THE ADVOCATE'S MEMORY (Book 13)
THE ADVOCATE'S NIGHTMARE (Book 14)
THE ADVOCATE'S OATH (Book 15)
THE ADVOCATE'S PHANTOM (Book 16)

THE TUPER MYSTERY SERIES

THE ADVOCATE'S FELONY

(Book 6 of The Advocate Series)
MASON'S MISSING (Book 1)
FINDING FRANKIE (Book 2)
RECOVERING RITA (Book 3)
LIBERATING LANA (Book 4)

CO-AUTHORED STANDALONE

NO CONSENT
(Co-authored with L.J. Sellers)

Chapter 1

Friday evening

Sabre sprinted as fast as she could. Her legs felt weak, and her bare feet hurt with every step, but she had to keep moving. The chilly night made her shiver. Wet from the blood covering her body, the air cut right through her. Terror filled her and made her run faster. *Would she make it?* She passed the 7-Eleven and darted across the street. Cars honked and screeched as she crossed in front of them. She passed El Portal Mexican Restaurant at the entrance to the shopping center parking lot and coached herself to keep going across the parking lot to Kohl's. Exhausted, she realized she couldn't maintain the pace much longer. Her body hit the side of the building as she tried to catch her breath. Sabre reached into her pocket for her phone, but it wasn't there. All she had for protection was a high-heeled shoe in her right hand.

A man parked twenty feet away got out of his car and strode toward her. She gripped the shoe as if it was her last hope, raising a hand to hit him if he came too close. When he was halfway to her, she flung the shoe. He sidestepped the flying pump, then stopped. Sabre took off.

"Hey," the man yelled.

"No!" Sabre shrieked and ran between the rows of parked cars. A vehicle suddenly backed out and knocked her down. Stunned but not seriously injured, she jumped up and kept running. She heard voices yelling behind her, but she didn't look back. *Keep going!* By the time she crossed the lot and reached Balboa, she had to slow down. Every step drew more strength than she thought she had. She stopped to catch her breath. Sabre heard a siren, then saw red lights coming her way. Two police cars pulled up beside her, and a policeman walked toward her.

"Help me," she moaned and collapsed to the ground.

Chapter 2

Saturday morning

Attorney Sabre Orin Brown woke up and glanced around at the sterile room. She was in a hospital, or at least she hoped she was. Groggy and confused, she tried to sit up. The pain in her head made her scowl. And the bottom of her feet hurt. She searched her memory for events that could have landed her here, but she was at a loss. She lay back against the pillow and closed her eyes, only to open them again when she heard the door.

"Good morning, sunshine." JP's voice was music to her ears, and the sight of his face made her smile. He wore his usual jeans, cowboy boots, and Stetson hat and carried a cup of coffee. He was her private investigator and for the past few years, her lover. They were, for all practical purposes, living together and raising his niece and nephew. And in a few days, her twelve-year-old cousin, Dené, would be living with them as well.

"I must look dreadful," Sabre said, and smoothed her hair back.

"You could look like Annie off the pickle boat, and you'd still be beautiful to me." He gently kissed her forehead.

Sabre smiled at the image. "What happened to me?" she asked. "Why am I here?"

"I was just about to ask you the same thing."

"I don't know."

"What's the last thing you remember?"

Sabre searched her brain. "I was headed to see a minor client in the Kearny Mesa area." She hesitated. "But I don't recall seeing her. I remember leaving my office and driving to Polinsky to see Dené and a new client I picked up yesterday. The child was no longer at the receiving home, and Dené had a therapy session, so I only stayed for a few minutes. After I left Polinsky, I drove in the direction of the foster home, but that's all I remember. Everything is foggy after that. Actually, it's blank."

"It's okay," JP said. "I'm sure it'll all come back to you."

Sabre looked at the bandages on her arm, then lifted the sheets. She had a few bandages on her right leg, several purple bruises, and a dull ache everywhere.

"Are you in a lot of pain?" JP asked.

"My stomach and head, mostly." Sabre looked at JP. "Do you know how I got here?"

"Yes. That much I know. The cops found you running down Balboa after leaving a shopping center on the corner of Balboa and Genesee. A witness said you got hit by a car pulling out of a parking space, but you bounced right back up and took off again."

"Is that how I got so beat up?"

"It might explain the scrapes on your arms and legs, but from what the witnesses said, you were already covered in blood and running scared. Can you remember anything about how you got to that parking lot?"

Sabre thought for a few seconds. "I have no idea." She looked into JP's eyes. He seemed more worried than he was letting on. "How long have I been here?"

"Overnight. This happened yesterday. The police are investigating, but they don't have much to go on."

"And I'm sure they have more important things to do."

"You have friends in the department."

"Who?"

"DuBois."

"You mean *you* have friends in the department."

"Same thing. DuBois and I go way back. We were on the beat together for quite a while. He's a good guy."

"I thought he planned to retire," Sabre said.

"Yeah, he keeps saying that, but he doesn't put in his notice. He'd be lost without his job. It's his life." JP smiled.

Sabre knew it was forced, that he was trying to make her feel at ease. "Is my phone here?"

"No, neither is your ID. You didn't have anything on you, no money, no cards, no driver's license. Nothing. They wouldn't have known who you were except that DuBois happened to be here when you arrived in the ambulance. He recognized you and called me."

"Please thank him for me."

"I will, but you can do that yourself. He'll be by to see you soon."

Sabre wrinkled her brow. "Did you say I was covered in blood?"

"Yes, your shirt was soaked. The police took it for evidence."

"Will you pull the covers off my feet, please?"

JP did as she'd asked.

"Why are my feet bandaged? The bottoms really hurt."

"Because you were barefoot. You were wearing that green top and flared skirt you like so much, the same clothes you wore to court yesterday."

"Dang. And they're ruined?"

"Both the shirt and skirt had blood on them, but the top was the worst, and the skirt was torn. That might have happened when you fell, but we can't be certain. We don't know when you took off your shoes. Most likely, you shed them so you could move faster. A witness said you were carrying one pump in the parking lot, then got spooked and threw it at him. The cops found that one, but they're still looking for the other one—and your car."

Chapter 3

Saturday morning

"Remember me?" Detective DuBois stepped into Sabre's hospital room and stood next to JP.

"Of course, I do." Sabre smelled the faint odor of cigarettes. She didn't remember that he smoked. What else had she forgotten? "Thanks for calling JP yesterday. It was nice having him here when I woke up." She realized the alternative scenario. "And he would've gone crazy waiting for me to come home last night."

"I'm just glad I saw you." DuBois glanced at JP. "McCloud's a good guy. I'd hate to have him worrying." DuBois always called him *McCloud* because JP had been wearing cowboy boots and a black Stetson when they were introduced and had reminded him of Dennis Weaver from the TV show *McCloud*.

JP walked to the window as they talked.

"But enough about him," DuBois said. "I understand you can't remember anything after leaving your office yesterday."

"Actually, I remember going to Polinsky and meeting for a few minutes with my cousin, but not much after that."

"Do you remember leaving Polinsky?"

"Yes," Sabre said. "I drove out of the parking lot, got on the freeway, and headed toward Kearny Mesa to see a child in the dependency system. She lives with an aunt just off of

Genesee. JP can get you the address from the file in my office. Or I can call Elaine. I'm sure she'd go there and get it for us."

"Who's Elaine?"

"My receptionist/secretary. If she's not busy, I'm sure she'd go."

"No need," JP said. "I can do it." Now he paced at the foot of her bed.

Sabre caught JP's attention. She wanted to tell him to calm down, but that would only irritate him. He needed to get out there and start finding some answers. "The file is on my desk, and the child's name is Angela Madison. It's a fairly simple case, so I can't imagine anyone in that family is involved."

"Is it a dependency case?" DuBois asked.

"Yes, long time drug history. Xander Madison, the child's mother, is in and out of rehab, and the aunt always steps up. The child is eight, and this is the third time she's been in the system. When the mother cleans up, she stays sober for a year or so, then fails again."

"Any history of violence?"

"No, nothing like that, just plain neglect."

"I'll check with the aunt and see if you ever made it to her house, and I'll put out a search in the area for your car. We've already canvassed around where you were found, but this might open it up more for us."

"Where exactly was I found?"

"On Balboa Avenue near the CVS drugstore," DuBois said.

"That's about a mile from where my client lives."

"We've pretty much covered that area, but we'll give it another look."

The door opened, and a short man in his early thirties walked in. "I'm Dr. Campbell," he said as he approached Sabre.

JP stopped pacing and moved closer to her bed.

"I'm Sabre. This is JP and Detective DuBois."

The doctor nodded. "Nice to meet you both. Have you determined what happened to my patient?"

"No," DuBois said, "but we will. Do you have anything that'll help?"

The doctor shined a light in Sabre's eyes and examined them, then turned to DuBois. "Not much. I know she took a hard blow to the head, and her stomach is bruised, but there is no apparent bleeding or damage to the organs that we can tell." He looked back at Sabre. "Are you able to remember anything more?"

"Nothing."

"Will she regain her memory?" JP asked.

"Maybe. Maybe not. The memory loss may be from the head trauma, in which case, a mild injury doesn't usually cause lasting amnesia. If the injury is too severe, it could be permanent. At this point, we don't know." The doctor glanced at the medical chart in his hands. "It doesn't appear to be that severe, but time will tell. We did an MRI and a CT scan to check for brain damage or abnormalities, and we found none. The blood tests didn't show an infection or nutritional deficiencies that might be the cause. Which means it was likely from whatever physical trauma she endured." He turned to Sabre. "Another possibility is dissociative amnesia, which stems from an emotional shock. Since we don't know what happened, we don't know if it's likely or not."

"Is that kind of amnesia permanent?" Sabre asked.

"Not usually, but there's no guarantee. If your memories return, they may be in pieces, or the whole thing may flood back at once. Again, it depends on the cause of the loss and whether something triggers your recall."

"Is there anything I can do to help?" Sabre asked.

"Just rest. Your body has been through quite an ordeal, maybe far worse than we know. It needs to recoup, and so does your brain."

"Can I go home? I can rest there easier."

"Not yet. We have an electroencephalogram scheduled to check for signs of seizure activity. If we rule that out, you can likely go home tomorrow."

"Thanks."

"I'll see you later." Dr. Campbell turned and left.

JP stepped close and gave her a quick kiss on the lips. "We'll go figure out what happened to you."

"Good idea. You're wearing a hole in the floor." She forced a smile. "Will you please call my mother and brother and make sure they understand I'm fine?"

"I already did. Ron's on his way back from Montana and will be here tomorrow."

"Did he cut his trip short because of me?"

"He was already on the road. Your mom will stop by a little later, and Bob is waiting outside. He'll be in as soon as we leave. And don't be alarmed, but there's a guard outside your door."

"Of course there is," Sabre said, a little miffed. "But that wasn't necessary, you know."

"Until we understand what happened, I'm not taking any chances. Since I can't be here to keep an eye on you, I took care of it." JP walked toward the door.

"JP, please be careful."

"Don't worry, darlin', I've got plenty of arrows in my quiver."

Chapter 4

Saturday morning

Bob Clark, Sabre's best friend, entered the room. "Hi, Sobs." He'd given her the nickname because her initials were S.O.B. They'd been friends since bonding over a difficult trial in juvenile court years ago.

Sabre pretended to search his face for clues, noticing his graying hair made him look older than his still-smooth face. "I'm sorry. Who are you?"

"What? My little S-O-B, how could you not know me? JP said you lost your memory of the events leading up to your hospitalization, but how could you not remember me?" He walked closer to her.

Sabre pulled back.

"Sobs, I'm your best friend."

Sabre smiled. "Yeah, I know. I'm just yanking your chain."

"That was mean."

"But fun. Come here. Give me a hug, but be gentle. I keep finding new aches and pains."

Bob hugged her gently. "You're a brat."

"I am, but you would've done the same."

"Probably." Bob pulled a chair toward the bed and sat down. "So, what cases can I handle for you?"

"I think the doctor will release me tomorrow. Today's Saturday, right?"

"Yes." Bob sounded hesitant.

"Well, if I'm released tomorrow, I can be back at work on Monday."

"Yeah," he paused. "I don't think so."

"Really. There's not that much wrong with me. I apparently had a blow to the head, but it doesn't seem to be that serious."

"*Apparently*, it's more serious than you think, or you wouldn't be talking about going back to work already."

"I'm really okay. My stomach hurts like someone used me as a punching bag, but the only other thing is my sore feet. I can wear tennis shoes or slippers or anything with a good cushion. I don't have any broken bones or anything serious. The doctor would've let me go today, but he decided to run a few more tests. If everything comes out okay, I'll be ready to go. Besides, I need to be home for Dené. She's coming to live with us on Monday."

"That can wait a day or two. She'll be fine."

"It's already been a big hassle getting the placement with JP and me. They don't say it, but I'm sure it's because we're not married. I could take Dené to my condo, but then I can't help with Conner and Morgan. We thought it would be best if we all stayed together. I just hope..."

"Sabre," Bob interrupted. "Do you have anything important on Monday's calendar?"

Sabre was worried. "I don't think so, but what if I do and I can't remember? I could have some high-profile case with a dozen kids living in squalor after years of abuse and neglect and the paparazzi waiting at my door."

"Sabre, you don't have a case like that. I would know."

"My point is, I can't know what I *don't* remember. I can only know what I *do* remember. Who knows what all I've forgotten?"

"Well, if that's the case, you shouldn't be doing hearings anyway. Did you check your calendar?"

"I don't have it. My planner is in my briefcase, which is in my car, which is still missing. I also have it on my phone, but it's gone too." Sabre realized she had a workaround. "My calendar is online too, so that's what you can do for me, bring me my computer."

"How about I bring it tomorrow if you're still here?"

Sabre lowered her head and raised her brows, looking at Bob with pleading eyes. "Come on. I don't have a phone or anything."

"There's one right there," Bob said, pointing to the hospital phone.

"But I hardly know anyone's number anymore. Besides, maybe I can help JP with his investigation, or get some work done while I'm here. And I'll check what I have on calendar for Monday in case I need your help."

"Okay, I'll go get it for you," Bob said. "I know you'll go stir crazy without it."

"Thanks, you're the best."

Chapter 5

Saturday morning

JP parked his truck behind Sabre's office and waited for DuBois. A few minutes later, the detective pulled in beside him and took a last drag from his cigarette before exiting his sedan. As they walked toward the back door, JP said, "I thought you quit smoking, DuBois."

"I have—many times. I quit for nearly ten years, then started again about six months ago. My wife is threatening to kill me if the smoking doesn't get me first. So, I'm thinking about giving it up again." He stopped before they reached the door. "Is someone in the office?"

JP noticed the door was ajar. "Sabre shares the office with two other attorneys, but there aren't any cars. Or it's possible Elaine could've come in for something and left."

They approached with caution, ready for any surprises. JP pulled his gun from his holster, but kept it lowered as he pushed open the door and called out, "David? Elaine? Is someone here?"

No one answered.

DuBois raised his Glock. "Police!"

Still nothing. They continued inside, JP in the lead, checking each room as they went. Satisfied they were alone, JP stepped into Sabre's office.

"Is it possible whoever left last, didn't lock the door?" DuBois asked.

"Not likely. Everyone here is pretty careful. We've had too many problems at this office in the past." JP searched Sabre's desk, but the file wasn't there. "Now that's strange. Sabre said the Madison case was on her desk."

"Maybe she forgot."

"That's not likely. She remembers everything in detail up until sometime after she left Polinsky. Besides, she's a creature of habit. When she's working on a file, she leaves it right here, unless she's going to court. When she returns, she puts her notes in the folder before she puts it away."

JP checked the cabinet but didn't find a folder labeled *Madison*. He holstered his weapon, then called Sabre's hospital room. When she picked up, he explained the situation. "Is it possible you took the file with you?"

"I remember putting it in the basket before I left, along with Dené's file and the Atkinson detention I picked up yesterday. It's not very big because it's new."

"There are no files in the basket or on your desk anywhere. I checked the cabinet for Madison, but it's not there either. Just a second." JP checked the drawers for the other two files. "They're not here either. If someone wanted a particular folder, why would they take all three?"

"In a hurry, maybe? I guess it's possible that I took them, but I have a distinct memory of putting them in the basket." Sabre paused. "But I don't trust myself right now."

"Don't beat yourself up too much. The door wasn't locked when we got here, so anything is possible."

"What? I know I locked it when I left. I distinctly remember Hugh went out the front and I went out the back. Something's not right. Call Hugh and see if he came back in, or maybe David."

"I'll do that next. In the meantime, is there any way to get the address we need?"

"I'll call Elaine. She's one of the few numbers I know by heart. She can look it up in our database, then I'll have her call your cell."

"I'll be in touch." JP hung up and turned to DuBois. "Let's go. We know which direction to head, and I'm sure Elaine will call shortly."

"Okay," the detective said. "I'll drive so you can make phone calls."

After checking to make sure the front door was locked, they went out the back and secured it as well. Then they climbed into DuBois' car and drove off. JP would have preferred to drive, but someone had assaulted Sabre, and finding the scumbag was his priority.

~~~

They were on the freeway heading north when Elaine called with the address. JP asked if she'd seen the Madison file, but the receptionist hadn't.

"Take the Genesee West offramp." He gave the address to DuBois, who asked Siri for directions. JP called Hugh, who claimed he left when Sabre did and hadn't returned to the office. JP then called David and left a message. David was seldom in the building since he rarely practiced law. He'd found a new business, selling ice cream cones.

Within a few minutes, they reached the condo complex where Angela Madison had been placed. As they exited the car, DuBois said, "I know it's difficult for you to hand over the reins, McCloud, but I need to take the lead here."

"Okay, boss."

"I mean it."

"I know. I'll keep quiet." JP smiled. "Unless you miss something."

DuBois shook his head and started for the front door. Before he knocked, he turned to JP. "What's the aunt's name?"

"Jan Webb."
~~~

A tall woman in her mid-forties answered, and DuBois showed her his badge. "I'm Detective Vincent DuBois, and this is a private investigator who works for Attorney Sabre Brown. Are you Jan Webb?"

"Yes. Come in."

They walked inside. She offered them a seat, but they both chose to stand.

"Is your niece, Angela Madison, here?" DuBois asked.

"She's upstairs. Do you need to talk to her?"

"We do, but first we have a couple of questions for you."

The aunt suddenly looked concerned. "Is Ms. Brown okay?"

"She is," DuBois said. "Did you see her last evening?"

"She called and made an appointment to come by, but she never showed. I tried calling her, but it went to voicemail."

"What time was the appointment?"

"Five o'clock. I waited until six, then I had to leave. I was pretty frustrated because I had some place to be. What's going on?"

"I apologize for her," JP said, "but the circumstances were beyond her control. Sabre's in the hospital, but she's doing okay. I'm sure she'll contact you soon."

"Oh my!" Jan's eyes widened. "What happened?"

"That's what we're trying to ascertain," DuBois said. "May we speak to Angela now?"

"Sure. I'll get her." Jan started for the stairs, then stopped. "Can I get either of you something to drink? I have water...and Pepsi. It's Angela's favorite, so I always keep some on hand."

"No, thank you," they both responded.

The woman returned a few minutes later with a bubbly girl who wore the brightest red pigtails JP had ever seen. It took him a few seconds to realize the hair was a wig and the freckles were fake.

As she approached, Angela reached out to shake hands. "Hi, I'm Anne with an E, but you can call me Angela if you want, because grown-ups like to do that."

"Sorry," Jan said. "She was playing dress up and insisted she come down as is. Anne of Green Gables is her favorite book and movie."

"No problem." JP smiled at the girl. "I love the pigtails."

"Thank you," Angela said. "I know red hair isn't very attractive, but I have to settle for what I have. When I'm grown up, I'll dye my hair. Maybe I'll be a blonde, or maybe I'll be a raven."

"Well, you look very cute," JP said. "I wanted to tell you that Ms. Brown is sorry she couldn't make it here yesterday."

"But she was here. Not in the house, but I saw her."

"Where?"

"I was upstairs in my room, and when I looked out the window, there she was."

"But she didn't come in?"

"No, I just waved to her, and then she left. But I don't think she saw me, because she didn't wave back."

Jan shook her head. "I'm afraid Angela likes to embellish things. As you can see by her costume, she lives in a bit of a fantasy world."

Chapter 6

Chapter 6

Saturday afternoon

"Hi, Sis." Ron smiled and walked into Sabre's hospital room. "I know you missed me and wanted me to come home, but pulling this stunt to get me here is a little over the top, don't you think?"

"You didn't have to hurry home for me," Sabre said. "I'm fine."

"I can see that." He kissed her forehead. "I was already on my way. I left Butte, Montana, early yesterday, and I drove to a motel in St. George, Utah. When JP called at 4:30 this morning, I got on the road and came straight here. That's normally what I do when I make the trip, except I left a few hours earlier than I might have, but that's all."

"How was your visit?"

"Pretty great, actually."

"How is Tuper?"

"He's Tuper, as ornery as ever. That man doesn't change much."

"And Clarice and Mary Ann?"

"They're both doing fine." Ron seemed to be suppressing a smile.

"What's up with you?"

"Nothing." Ron still looked sheepish.

"What's up with you?"

"Lana and I helped Tuper with a case. We spent time in the Hutterite Colony again. It was nice seeing all of them."

"You and Lana? The hacker?"

"Yes." Ron broke into a grin.

"You like her," Sabre said, her voice teasing. "You've fallen for Lana."

"Don't be silly."

"What's she like?" Sabre felt like she was chatting with a middle-school girlfriend. "I've talked to her a couple of times, but she has always been all business. Is she cute?"

"She's okay," Ron said.

Sabre tipped her head. "Come on."

"Okay, she's adorable, spunky, and sometimes a real pain in the ass, but she's fascinating. She has short, red spiked hair, and she wears combat boots. She doesn't care what others think about her, yet she has a soft spot for animals and for Tuper. She doesn't trust most people, but when she does, she's loyal. She's also funny and—"

"Wow!" Sabre interrupted. "You're smitten, big brother."

"You didn't let me finish. She's also seventeen hours away."

"Only three by air." Before Ron could say more, she asked, "When are you going to see her again?"

"Probably never. I have work to do with Aunt Goldie's trust. I need to find a recipient and do a good deed for her."

"There's no timetable on that, and you can do it from anywhere."

"When are you getting out of here?" Ron asked.

"Okay, I'll change the subject—for now. I should be out tomorrow. They have more tests to run, but I'm ready to go *now*."

"I talked to JP, and he said you can't remember what happened."

"Not a thing. The doctor said the memory may or may not come back."

"I'm headed home to clean up, then I'll bring Mom by here. She wanted to come earlier, but I guess she felt better once she talked to you. I offered to help JP with the investigation, but he said he was working with DuBois and would let me know if he needed anything. Meanwhile, I'll keep you company so he can do his job."

"You don't need to babysit me. I'm fine. Get going so Mom can come here. I need to see her too. Bob will be back soon with my laptop, and that'll give me something to do."

"All right, Sis." He squeezed her hand. "I guess you're safe while you're here. I'll be back in a couple of hours."

As soon as Ron left, Sabre called JP. He told her about his visit with Angela.

"She could be making up a story. She loves to do that. Did she say she saw anything else?"

"No, that was pretty much it."

"I need to talk to her myself. I may be able to get more information out of her and figure out if she's being truthful."

"Do you want me to bring her to you?"

"No, that's not a good idea."

"I suppose that might scare her. I'm sorry. I'm just thinking of you and want to catch whoever did this."

"Actually, I doubt it would bother her." Sabre had gotten to know Angela after a few visits. "She's an interesting girl, and I think the hospital setting would prompt her to embellish her story. Maybe I can talk to her tomorrow."

"We'll see. In the meantime, we have a few more leads to follow up on. I'm checking on Todd Lynch."

"Do you really think he might have done this?"

"I don't know, but I'm not leaving any stone unturned. That man blames you for everything that ever went wrong in his life. He's always a suspect. When you get your computer, maybe you can go through your cases and see if anything triggers a suspect for us."

"I will, but the assault could be totally random."

"Still, we'll do our best to track your steps." He paused. "By the way, they found your car. DuBois and I are headed there now. Technicians will check it for fingerprints and anything else that might give us a clue."

"Where is it?"

"In Tecolote Canyon near Boyd and Acworth Streets. Some hikers found it."

"That's not far from Angela's house," Sabre said, visualizing the area. But once again she had no memory of being there.

Chapter 7

Saturday afternoon

JP and DuBois drove into the canyon where Sabre's car had been found. The dirt road continued, but several patrol vehicles were parked alongside, and a policeman stopped them before they could go any further.

When DuBois showed his badge and identified himself, the cop instructed them to pull over and walk the rest of the way. JP climbed out and followed DuBois toward the trees and brush but didn't see Sabre's car. He heard voices in the distance and saw two men measuring tire tracks alongside the road.

"How did you get so much manpower on this?" JP asked.

"I've been around a while and besides, you're one of us."

"Thanks, man. I really appreciate it."

Before they got very far, a tall, African-American man in his late thirties approached. "You must be McCloud," he said.

"JP, actually." He extended his hand.

"This is my partner, Bryce Erickson," DuBois said.

"Sorry about your girlfriend. How's she doing?"

"She'll be okay," JP said. "Thanks for asking."

"Where's the car?" DuBois asked.

"Right over here." Bryce walked toward the bushes. "They just finished fingerprinting, so we can get a closer look now."

At first glance, the BMW didn't look too bad, but as they got closer, JP saw several dents and scratches. He walked around to the front and discovered a broken headlight and smashed grill. In the back, the trunk was wide open.

"Was it open when they found the car?" JP asked.

"Yes," Erickson said. "And it was completely empty. It's hard to know if the perp left it that way, or if someone else discovered the car after it was abandoned." He glanced at the hollow space. "Did Sabre usually keep things in her trunk?"

"Not a lot. Just an emergency first-aid kit, several bottles of water, and usually her briefcase."

"What about her purse?"

"She doesn't carry one."

"Seriously? I've never known a woman who didn't carry a purse."

DuBois and Erickson searched the inside of the car. JP stood back and let them do their jobs. He would take a quick look after they finished. Erickson picked up a Styrofoam coffee cup from the ground near the passenger side. "This looks like it hasn't been here long. Perhaps it fell out of the car."

"That's not Sabre's," JP said.

"How do you know?" DuBois asked.

"Because she won't drink out of Styrofoam. She says it feels like nails on a chalkboard and it ruins the taste. Besides, she has this whole 'bad for the environment' thing going on."

Erickson bagged the cup for evidence.

Very little was found in the car. No phone. No briefcase. No paperwork, except for a two-month-old Thai-food receipt that DuBois found under the passenger seat.

While the detectives finished up, JP looked around the area, being careful not to disturb the terrain. He had only gone about twenty feet when Erickson joined him.

"Find anything?"

"Just more dried bushes and a few animal droppings." They continued on.

"Oh, no! DuBois!" Erickson called out. "Something over here you have to see."

JP stepped up and within seconds, DuBois joined them. "What the hell?"

Erickson was leaning over the body of an African-American man in a blue sweatshirt and jeans, both covered in blood. The detective felt for a pulse. "He's been dead a while."

"Check his body for ID," DuBois said. "I'll call it in."

Erickson searched the corpse. "There's nothing in his pockets."

"We found a body near the car in Tecolote Canyon," DuBois said into his phone. "African-American male, approximately thirty-five years old, no identification. He has a large gash on his head, and a gunshot in his chest. Lots of blood on his person as well as the ground around his head and upper body." He stopped for a moment to listen. "No, I can handle it."

DuBois hung up and approached JP. "Things are getting sticky. You know we have to compare the blood on Sabre with this body."

JP felt a flicker of fear. "What are you saying?"

"You can't work with me until she's cleared. I'll do what I can to keep you in the loop, but you know how this goes."

"Yeah, everyone becomes a suspect, and Sabre is on that list now."

"It would help if she could remember what happened, especially now that I'm officially assigned this case."

"You'll be the first to know if she gets her memory back." JP took photos of the body and started to walk away, then stopped. "DuBois, I know Sabre couldn't do this unless it was self-defense, and even then, it would be hard for her to kill a man."

"Maybe that's why she can't remember it."

Chapter 8

Sunday morning

When Sabre walked in the door, both kids hurried over. Conner, who was not yet sixteen years old, took her arm. "Let me help you," Conner said. Sabre looked up at him, now a tall, lanky man. He'd changed so much in the few months she'd known him. He had filled out a lot, and his short haircut made him look older. Like his father and Uncle JP, he was handsome.

"Do you want to sit down?" Eleven-year-old Morgan asked. "Would you like something to eat or drink?"

"Kids, I'm fine," Sabre said. "I'm a little sore, but that's it."

"Can I hug you?" Morgan asked.

"Of course." Sabre reached out for the little girl in round, red glasses, whose big brown eyes were filled with compassion. Morgan held on tighter than was physically comfortable, but Sabre didn't complain. When the girl finally let go, Sabre said, "I'm really okay. I just have some scrapes and bruises. They'll heal in no time."

Conner reached down and gave Sabre a quick hug. "We're glad you're okay."

"Me too."

"She really is fine," Ron said. "There's no need to worry. Now, what do you have to eat? I'm starving."

"I made a pot of Dad's chili," Morgan said.

"No beans," Sabre and Ron said at the same time.

"That's right. Dad always says"—Morgan lowered her voice—"no self-respecting man would put beans in his chili."

By the time they finished eating, the kids were convinced Sabre was, in fact, all right, so they started doing their own things. Morgan went to her room, and Conner went for a bike ride with a friend. Sabre liked that Conner still enjoyed riding. It seemed to keep him younger, and it saved on gas.

Sabre and Ron were discussing a car rental when Morgan came back to the living room with Louie, JP's beagle, following close behind. She had changed from sweats into a pair of jeans and a pink shirt.

"You look nice," Sabre said.

"I am supposed to go to Erin's birthday party today, but I don't have to. I know there's a lot going on, and I can call her and tell her I can't make it. It's okay, really. I don't mind. I can stay here with you and keep you company."

She is such a sweet girl, and quite the social butterfly. It seems as if she gets an invitation to a birthday party every week. Sabre smiled. "Go to the party. I don't need a babysitter. Besides, Ron's taking me to rent a car so I have something to drive until I get mine back." Sabre checked the time. "We can drop you at the party on the way." She turned to her brother. "Right, Ron?"

"Absolutely."

A huge smile crossed Morgan's face. "I just have to grab her present." She ran back to her room.

Sabre pulled out the new phone they'd picked up on the way home. A message from JP. She opened it and shuddered at the photo he'd sent.

"What's that?" Ron asked.

"A body they found in the canyon near my car."

"Do you know him?"

"I sure don't. At least I think I don't."

~~~
~~~

After they rented a car, Ron went home, and Sabre planned to conduct a home visit to see Angela Madison. She was still in the parking lot when JP called. He wasn't happy with her update.

"Dammit, Sabre. That's what started this whole thing. How do you know it won't happen again?"

"I don't, but I can't stop doing my job. And I won't live in fear."

"Here we go again."

"What does that mean?"

"It means you take too many chances. My job is supposed to be the dangerous one, but you're at risk more than I am."

"I can't help that."

"You can be more careful." JP raised his voice, which he seldom did, but quickly apologized. "I'm sorry, Sabre. I just get scared. I can't lose you. And even if you're safe, going there might jog your memory. Since we have no idea what that might entail, I'd really like to be with you." He paused, but not long enough for her to cut in. "Look, I'm done here. Why don't I meet you at home, and we'll go together? It would make me feel a lot better."

Sabre hesitated, then said, "Sure. I'll see you in a few." After she hung up, she felt relieved. Until JP brought up the risk she was taking, she hadn't given it much thought. She was so used to forging forward, regardless of the consequences. Now she had more people to think about. Besides JP, she had Conner and Morgan, whom she'd really bonded with, and soon Dené would be part of her life as well. Sabre had concerns about her cousin's nearly twelve-year-old daughter coming to live with them, but she couldn't turn her away.

Sabre drove home and went out to the patio to wait for JP. It was a beautiful October day in San Diego, warmer than it had been the last week. The sun was shining, and the seventy-five-degree air was still. Sabre sat down in a lounge chair and fell asleep. She was far more tired than she had realized earlier. She woke up when JP called out her name. She cleared her throat and tried not to sound sleepy. "Were you sleeping?" He stepped outside.

"Resting mostly. I might have dozed off, but I'm ready to go." Sabre stood up.

"If you want to rest, I can go alone," JP said.

"Nope, let's go."

~~~

Angela wore a light blue princess dress and a tiara in her dark brown curls. The girl perched on the edge of her bed, looking regal. Sabre sat down next to her, but JP stayed on his feet.

"It's very important, Angela, that you tell me the truth." Sabre used her quiet-but-firm tone. "Did you see me on Friday?"

"Yes, I did, Ms. Brown."

"Tell me exactly what you saw."

"I was watching out the window. I like to do that. I watch to see what is going on in the neighborhood."

"Where were you standing?"

Angela walked over to the corner windows that gave her a great view. "I was right here," she said. "I can see a lot from up here. See that house across the street?" She pointed at a condo with a blue garage door.

Sabre walked over.

"That kid goes fishing all the time. He's always taking his fishing pole and putting it in the car, then his dad drives him somewhere. I've never seen him bring any fish in though, unless they're in the cooler or something. And that house next door to it." Angela gestured again. "There's an older lady that lives there. Her man friend comes to see her, and they stand out on the porch and hug and kiss. But first, he goes out by himself and smokes a cigarette. She's never out there when he's smoking. I figure she probably doesn't like the smoke."
~~~

"And this is exactly where you were standing when you saw me?"

"Yes."

"Where was I?"

"I saw you drive up, and you parked right there across from Fishing Boy's house."

"Did you see me get out of the car?"

"I didn't see you actually get out because I was watching a cute little white dog over there." She pointed up the street. "But then I looked back, and you were walking from the back of your car to the driver's side. I waved to you."

"Did I wave back?"

"No, you weren't looking up here. The next time I checked, you were gone." Angela walked away from the window.

"Wait a minute, please. I have a few more questions," Sabre said.

Angela turned back. "Okay."

"Did you see anyone with me?"

"No, but they could've been in the car, and I wouldn't have seen them."

"Did you see me leave?" Sabre asked.

"No. I thought you had come into my house, so when I couldn't see you anymore, I went back to my dolls and waited for you. I was having a tea party. I knew it would be a while before my aunt came to get me because she always talks to you before we talk."

"You mean my car was gone?"

"No. I could still see your car, but not you."

"Was I inside the car?"

"I don't know. I couldn't see you if you were."

"So, you didn't see me after I walked from the trunk toward the driver's door?"

"No, I went back to the window a while later, but your car was gone, so I figured you weren't visiting me."

"I need you to think carefully," Sabre said. "Did you see anyone else besides me and the dog?"

"A woman was walking the dog, but they disappeared around the corner pretty quick. And there was a man sitting on that rock over there." She pointed to a landscaped area in front of the complex. "But he was there before you got here."

"How long before?"

"I don't know. I looked out once before I saw you, and he was there."

"What was he doing?"

"Just sitting there. Doing nothing."

"Was he alone? Did he have a dog with him, maybe?"

"No, he was alone."

"Can you tell me what he looked like?"

"I couldn't see him very well, but he was dark."

"It was dark? Or, he was dark?"

"He was dark skinned, but I don't know if he was a black man or not. He just looked dark."

"Was he young or old?"

"Older than Fishing Boy, but younger than the old guy who smokes."

"Did you notice what he was wearing?" JP asked.

"A blue sweatshirt and jeans, I think."

Chapter 9

Chapter 9

Monday morning

In the attorney lounge at juvenile court, Sabre picked up her reports. A moment later, Bob walked in, scowling. "Are you sure you should be here?"

"Good morning to you, too."

"I don't know if getting back to work so soon is a good idea."

"I'm fine, *Mom*," Sabre said, drawing out the word.

Bob stared hard.

"Really. I'm okay." Sabre handed him a new detention sheet. "Look what we got on calendar this morning."

Bob's face lit up. "I want the mother on this one."

"I figured you would."

Bob read through the report. "This is bitchin'."

"I'm glad you're so excited at the plight of my client."

"You know better than that. It's just good to get something different for a change."

"I have to agree with you there."

"I'm off to find my client," Bob said. "I'll see you in a few."

Sabre followed him out, then turned toward Department Three. She did a sentencing hearing for a delinquent client, and when she came out of the courtroom, Bob was waiting for her.

"Did you meet your new client?" Sabre asked.

"Yes, and she seems like an amiable woman. A little high-strung but very concerned about her son, Eddie."

Sabre raised an eyebrow.

"I've always wanted one of these cases. They're so rare." Bob and Sabre walked down the hall toward Department Four as he talked. "I think there has only been one other filed here since we started in juvenile court."

"Thank goodness," Sabre said. "This is tragic. How can anyone do this sort of thing?"

"Hey, Sobs, we don't know that she did it. She's been accused, but the Department of Social Services could be wrong. You're supposed to have an open mind."

"You're right," Sabre said. "But did you see the photos?"

"Yes, the boy is very thin and pale. He's sick. She knows that."

"You read the report. The kid has been treated for everything imaginable. And Eddie says his mother gives him 'special medicine.'"

"Doctors make mistakes, too," Bob countered. "Lots of them. Munchausen by Proxy is a serious allegation. What if the mother is *not* projecting her weird kind of crazy on this kid? What if he really is sick but the doctors can't diagnose it?"

"Then I guess we'll have to find the problem." She gave him a half smile. "And they don't call it Munchausen anymore. It's Factitious Disorder."

"I know, but Munchausen sounds so much more interesting. It has a nice ring, don't you think?" Bob opened the door for Sabre, then followed her inside the courtroom. He continued to mutter, "Munchausen. Munchausen."

"You're sick."

"Of course he is," Deputy Mike McCormick commented. "You're excited about getting the new case, aren't you?"

"Of course I am," Bob said. "It's different. And watch, I'll win this."

"Yeah, I doubt that." Mike returned to his desk.

"Side bet? Lunch?" Bob grinned.

"You're on," Mike said.

"I heard that," Judge Hekman said, as she walked in. "Please don't do that."

"Just messing around, Your Honor," Bob said. "We'd never actually bet on the outcome of a case."

"No, of course you wouldn't." Hekman, a gray-haired woman, shook her head and took the bench.

"In re the Eddie Blane case," the clerk said.

Judge Hekman appointed Sabre to represent the child, Eddie Blane, and Bob for the mother, Willow Blane. Despite Bob's impassioned plea for the child to be detained with the mother upon his release from the hospital, the judge ordered foster home placement and supervised visits.

"One more thing, Your Honor," Sabre said. "I would ask that the order for detention be in a medically fragile home. At this point, we don't know what this child's condition is, or what the cause is, but I believe it is in his best interest to have someone who is used to dealing with ill children."

"There may be a family available, Your Honor," County Counsel Dave Casey said. "We would like to evaluate any potential homes with discretion to detain."

"So ordered with minor's attorney's concurrence," Hekman said.

After the mother left the courtroom, Judge Hekman called Sabre to the bench.

She wasn't sure what to expect, but stepped forward.

"Are you okay?" the judge asked in a soft voice. "I heard what happened."

"I wish someone would tell me, because I can't remember a thing."

"I just meant that I heard about your incident. Should you be home resting? You look pretty beat up."

Just like Hekman to not hold back. "I'm a little sore, but nothing permanent—I hope. I'm okay. This is my last hearing, so I'll be leaving after this. Thanks for your concern."

Sabre and Bob walked out.

"Are you going home?" Bob asked.

"I have to pick up Dené from Polinsky, and then I'm going home. If I'm up to it, I'll visit Eddie in the hospital later today."

"Are you sure you should be alone? Since we have no idea what happened, you could be in danger. What if you saw something you shouldn't have, and someone intends to finish the job?"

"You're so dramatic." Sabre studied the concern on his face. "Look, I'm okay. I'm being careful, and I would bet money that JP has Ron lurking close by. I know JP would be with me himself if he wasn't busy investigating."

"I'll walk you out," Bob said.

Sabre tipped her head and gave him a disconcerting look, then decided to let it go. He would do it anyway whether she argued or not.

On the way to her car, Sabre handed Bob her phone, displaying the photo JP had sent.

"Is this the dead guy in the canyon?" Bob asked.

"That's him. Does he look familiar?"

"No. Should he?"

"I just thought if he was someone who had been to court, you might recognize him."

Bob pushed his glasses up on his forehead and squinted. "I don't think I've ever seen him."

"Yeah, me either." Sabre got in her car, but before she backed out, Bob knocked on the window. She rolled it down just as her phone beeped.

"Happy Birthday, Sobs."

Sabre read her text. "Oh, yeah, thanks."

"What's wrong?"

"Nothing really." She showed the text to Bob. "The cops found my other shoe in the bushes on the corner of Boyd and Genesee."

Chapter 10

Monday morning

JP sat in Sabre's office trying to figure out what to do next. He had to find some clue as to what had happened to her. He didn't like leaving Sabre alone, but he knew Bob would keep an eye on her while she was at court. JP read through the Angela Madison case three times, but nothing popped out. The mother had been in and out of jail for possession with intent to sell drugs and prostitution, and the father's whereabouts were unknown. He hadn't been in the picture since Angela was a baby. The first time the mother went to jail, the girl had been two and a half. Her mother served six months, then went to work at a Burger King and stayed clean for a little over two years. At least it appeared so. She lost her job and hit the streets again, then was arrested, convicted, and served a year. Her last period of sobriety lasted less than a year before she was arrested again. No wonder Angela lived in a fantasy world. Her reality wasn't manageable.

JP thumbed through other cases that might have someone with a motive to hurt Sabre. Most were dead ends, but one delinquency file had a pretty angry father. JP set it aside for further investigation, then pulled out the old Lynch file. Todd Lynch was always a suspect. He had been stalking and harassing Sabre for years after she represented his three boys. Their mother was a druggie, and Lynch was the non-offending parent, but he had serious anger issues.

Sabre hadn't been on the case very long before the children were placed in a home in Pasadena and the case transferred to Los Angeles. But Todd Lynch still continued to harass Sabre with letters, emails, and social media posts. As recently as a few weeks ago, he'd sent her another threatening note.

JP called DuBois and reminded him about Lynch. "He seems to be all broth and no beans. But he's worth checking out again. I can do that, but I wanted you to be aware of it, in case something comes up."

"I appreciate that, McCloud. I read through the Madison file I obtained from DSS and found nothing suspicious. We've got a search out for the father, but finding him seems highly unlikely."

"I did the same, and I agree about the father." JP picked up the file he'd set aside. "I found a delinquency case that's worth checking out. The kid committed assault and battery with a hate crime enhancement. No surprise—he had an angry father. Sabre represented the teenager, Waylon Holloway, who beat up another kid for wearing a pink shirt to school. Sabre argued to keep the case in juvenile court. The DA wanted to send it downtown. She even had to fight the father on that. He claimed his sixteen-year-old son was a man and could handle himself in the big house if that's what happened. He also told her that if she did her job, his kid would walk."

"What a jerk."

"For sure. Sabre tried to settle the case with awareness programs and probation. I did a little work on the case, and I remember Waylon wanted to plead out, but once the father intervened, the kid refused to take the deal. They lost the trial, and the father was angry at everyone, but Sabre was at the top of his list."

"Send me the details, and I'll do some follow-up."

"Hey," JP said, "if you go see Holloway's father, I'd like to come along."

DuBois was silent for a few seconds. "We'll see. And, McCloud, don't go there on your own. I can't have you interfering with my investigation."

"Then take me with you."

"I'll call you after I do a background on the father."

JP switched gears. "Did you get the identity of the dead guy near Sabre's car?"

"He's still a John Doe. If the guy has a record, it's not in California, but we're branching out. Hopefully, we'll have something soon." DuBois hung up.

JP called a policeman who lived next door to Todd Lynch. "Hi, Rick, it's JP Torn. Remember me?"

"Of course, you're the one who has trouble with my *wonderful* neighbor. What can I do for you?"

"Have you seen Lynch lately?"

"Not for about a week. Are you having more trouble with him?"

"I'm not sure." JP explained what had happened to Sabre.

"I'm sorry to hear that," Rick said. "Lynch is always my first suspect too when anything strange happens around here. Is there anything I can do for you?"

"Not at this point. I may make a home visit to see his mother."

"Mother Dearest. She's a piece of work. I guess it's no wonder Todd is the way he is."

JP hung up and went back to reading case files. There had to be something in one of them. But there was a possibility the assault had nothing to do with her court work, which would make the investigation even harder. He kept reading until Detective DuBois called him back.

"We found Sabre's other shoe," DuBois said. "It matched the one we have, and I sent Sabre a photo and she confirmed it. We're trying to track the route she ran that night. Maybe you can help with that."

"I'd be glad to."

"I'll send you a map of the route we've charted so far, and you can take it from there."

"I'll get right on it."

"I learned a few things about Waylon's father, Gunner Holloway," DuBois added. "He's an equal opportunity racist who spouts online hate about Jews, Blacks, Mexicans, and gays. It doesn't matter which minority; he has posted something negative about them all. Facebook recently banned him after some pretty ugly statements. Not that it did much good; he just found other sites to spew his hate on. Holloway has also been active in demonstrations across the country the past few years. For some reason, he seems particularly threatened by the gay and lesbian community."

"What a sweetheart," JP said. "Any criminal record?"

"Some domestic violence, but the calls were made by neighbors, and the wife always denied the problem, so no convictions. And fifteen years ago, he served time in Texas for assault and battery. It was a bar fight, and Gunner left two guys in pretty awful shape. He has a few other arrests, but he lawyers up quickly and most of it seems to go away." DuBois paused. "What's the kid like?"

"Sabre says Waylon was surprisingly contrite until his father got to him. He wouldn't or couldn't explain why he hurt that other kid, but other boys were egging him on, especially his brother. When I saw him, he tried to act tough, but I don't think he really is. If it's okay with Sabre, I might pay him a visit in Urban Camp."

"Good idea."

"In the meantime," JP asked, "can we go see Gunner?"

"Okay, but McCloud, I'm doing the questioning."

"I never miss a good chance to shut up."

"Right."

Chapter 11

onday afternoon

Sabre walked into the Polinsky building, nervous about bringing Dené home. But she had agreed to do so and would keep her promise. The offer had seemed like a good idea at the time, but now she wasn't sure. Another child in the house, one she didn't really know, triggered some anxiety. She had decided years ago that she wouldn't have any children, and now she was helping raise three. Conner and Morgan had turned out to be easier than she'd expected. They were quite independent and had obviously fended for themselves growing up. But overall, they still took a lot of energy, something she was in short supply of right now. They were JP's family, and he had stepped up to do a lot more parenting than she'd expected. She knew he would help with Dené as well, but the emotional stuff and real responsibility would all be on her with this child.

A few minutes later, a staff member brought a stunning, tall, blonde girl into the lobby. She was carrying a small bag with her belongings. Dené had experienced so much loss in such a short time. First, her mother passed away, then her grandmother, and until recently, she hadn't even met her father. But now that she had, she needed time to get to know him. Taking her in was the right thing to do. When she got to know her father better, she would likely go live with him. Until then, Sabre would do what she could for her.

"You ready?" Sabre asked.

"I am." Dené was quiet until they reached the car. When she got inside, she asked, "Will I be able to get my other stuff from my old house?"

"Your father already brought over your personal things and clothes, but not your bed and dresser. He wasn't sure exactly what you wanted, and we didn't have room for everything. But everything you had with your mom is stored at your dad's house until you need it."

"That's okay."

"You'll get a chance to go through your belongings and see what you need."

Dené tried to smile, but she looked sad. On the drive home, Sabre wondered if the girl was thinking about her mother. Her life had been completely uprooted. And now she was about to be mingled into an already unusual family situation with people she had never met. Dené had been scheduled to spend a Saturday with them weeks ago, but she'd gotten sick and hadn't come. So, this would be her first introduction to everyone except Sabre.

As they got out of the car, Conner came out and offered to help.

"You can grab her bag. This is Dené, by the way." Sabre nodded toward Conner. "And this is Conner, the young man I told you about."

"Hi." Dené shuffled her feet and avoided eye contact.

"Welcome to our home." Conner took the bag out of the trunk and started toward the house.

Sabre and Dené followed. "We were just talking about school," Sabre said.

"What grade are you in?" Conner asked, as they walked inside.

"Seventh."

"I was about to tell Dené that, for now, she can have her choice of schools." Sabre turned to the girl. "If you want to finish out the semester at your old school, that's fine. Or, you can go to the middle school nearby."

"I'd like to stay with my friends."

"Then that's what we'll do."

Conner said little, but he kept glancing at Dené. Sabre wondered what he was thinking. *Was he concerned that he would have another sister to look after? Conner was very protective of Morgan.* "Will you pick up Morgan from school?" Sabre asked.

"Yeah, sure," Conner said. "Bye."

Sabre and Dené walked down the hall to the first bedroom. "I'm afraid we don't have another room for you," Sabre said. "You'll have to share with Morgan for now."

Dené glanced around. "It's pretty, but..."

"What is it?"

"There's only one bed. Where will I sleep?"

"But it's a big bed. I'm afraid you'll have to share for now. If this doesn't work, we can talk about getting bunk beds, or maybe we can fit two twins in here." Sabre walked to the closet and opened the door. "Your clothes are all here, and you have three drawers in the dresser. Morgan moved her things out and gave you the top drawers."

"I'm sorry. I didn't mean to sound ungrateful. It's just that I've always had to share a bed with my mom, which I'd be glad to do now if I could." Dené cleared her throat. "I was hoping I'd have my own room or at least my own bed." She sighed. "But it might be fun having other kids around. I've never had siblings."

"Conner and Morgan are pretty easy going. I think you'll all get along."

Sabre heard the front door open and within seconds, Morgan was in the room. Sabre introduced the girls.

"Hi, Dené. Welcome. You'll like it here. Uncle Johnny is a hoot, and Sabre is really nice. You'll have to get used to my uncle's funny sayings, though. He says a lot of funny stuff.

But they both take real good care of us, and they let us get involved in school activities. Conner doesn't join much, but I enjoy doing things. I'm in gymnastics right now, and that's a lot of fun. You seem pretty mature, so you might think gymnastics is too young for you, but I'm sure you'll find something you like to do. You are beautiful, by the way." Morgan kept talking without a pause. "Actually, you're more than beautiful. You're picturesque. Maybe I didn't use that word right. You're like perfect. Your hair is amazing."

Sabre interrupted. "Is picturesque your word of the day?" Morgan practiced a new unfamiliar word every day, and everyone in the house tried to help her if she misused it.

"Yes, but I didn't expect to use it on Dené. It seems to fit though. Right?"

"Picturesque certainly describes her, although, I think it's more often used with objects than people."

"Well, I wish I looked like you," Morgan said, looking at Dené. "I'm skinny and clumsy, and I have to wear these glasses. Sometimes the kids make fun of my glasses, but at least they're red. I like red. And my hair is this mousy brown color. Yours is like spun gold. When I'm older, I'll be able to get contacts, and maybe I can dye my hair. We'll see. I am getting taller, so maybe that'll help."

When Morgan finally paused, Dené jumped in. "Thank you for your compliments, but you're very pretty yourself. The truth is, I don't feel all that pretty. It's hard to see our own strengths sometimes, I guess. That's probably why you don't know how beautiful you are. And I love your glasses."

Sabre took a deep breath. *Maybe this would work after all.* She was concerned about Conner's reaction, however. He already spent most of his life taking care of Morgan. He didn't need another "sister" he felt responsible for. Both she and JP had tried to give Conner a more normal home life. She knew bringing Dené into the mix would change the dynamics, but she hoped it was for the better. Now she wasn't so sure.

Her thoughts were interrupted when Ron walked in the door. "Why isn't your door locked?"

"I thought it was. Morgan must've left it open when she came in."

"You need to talk to her."

"I will, but she's usually good about locking the door. She was just excited to meet Dené." Sabre tipped her head inquisitively. "What are you doing here anyway?"

"I wanted to make sure you were okay. Can't a man check on his favorite sister?"

"I'm your only sister."

"And that's why you're my favorite."

Chapter 12

Chapter 12

Monday afternoon

JP and DuBois walked up to the mobile home. It sat in a small park in El Cajon with about twenty trailers, a couple of which looked unoccupied. Car parts and cans of drained oil sat on the front patio. DuBois knocked on the door.

A full-bodied woman in her forties, wearing a loose-fitting dress and no makeup, answered the door. "What?" she said.

DuBois pulled his badge. "Detective DuBois. Are you Mrs. Holloway?"

"Yes, why?"

"Is your husband home, ma'am?"

"No."

"I'd like to ask a few questions."

"No, thank you."

She started to close the door, but DuBois kept talking. "Do you know when Gunner will be home?"

"Nope."

This time, she didn't wait for more questions. She shut the door, and they heard the lock click.

"That went well," JP said. "Now what?"

"You got some time?"

"Probably more than you do."

"Let's wait a while. According to the information I got, if Gunner's at work, he could be home any time now. If not, we'll go check out his place of employment."

"Which is?"

"He works as a mechanic for a big trucking company."

They moved the car, so it was out of sight of the trailer, but they could see anyone who entered or left the park. While they waited, they talked about this case and what to do next.

"What did you learn from the tracks around Sabre's car?" JP asked.

"It appears her vehicle was the only one there, at least that went off the road. Trucks that belong to the golf course go through there occasionally, but they stay on the road. So, if someone else was present, their vehicle didn't get close to the body."

Several cars came and went while they waited. Finally, a blue Ford F-150 pickup pulled in.

"That's him," DuBois said.

They waited until he passed, then followed him to the trailer. DuBois was out of the car almost before Gunner stepped out of his truck. JP bolted after him.

"Gunner Holloway?" the detective said.

"Yeah, what do you want?"

"To ask a few questions." He flashed his badge. "Detective DuBois, and this is JP."

"Can it wait? I'm hungry and tired." He was covered in black grease and appeared to have just gotten off work.

"Now would be good."

Gunner leaned against his truck. The man was tall and muscular, except for the extra weight around his middle. "What do you want to know?"

"Could we go inside and talk?"

"You can say what you want here. You already have my son, so if it's about him, there's nothing left to say."

"Where were you on Friday night around six o'clock?"

"Home with my wife, or at the bar shooting pool, or maybe I was in church. I'm not sure. That was three days ago, but I could check my social calendar if it's that important to you."

JP wanted to punch the guy. His lack of respect for law enforcement was hard to swallow.

"It's that important to me." DuBois' voice was firm, but mellow, showing little emotion. "If this isn't working for you, we can go down to the police station and finish the questioning. Perhaps you can think better there."

JP liked the way DuBois handled him. *The old man still had it.*

Gunner ran a hand through his light brown hair, exposing his receding hairline. "I was home with my wife. I remember now. She made fish sticks or some crap like that. She still cooks fish on Friday. I can't seem to break her of her childhood habits. Why do you want to know? What are you trying to pin on me?"

"We're just following up a lead. Can we talk to your wife so she can corroborate your story?"

"It's not a story, and she's not home right now."

"That's funny. She was there a few minutes ago," DuBois said.

"Well, she's gone now. You must've scared her off. She doesn't like your kind much."

"My kind? What is that?"

"Cops. They always try to trick her into saying I hurt her. I don't hurt the woman. That wouldn't be right now, would it?"

"I just want to verify your statement, then we'll be on our way."

"She's not here." Gunner pointed toward the trailer. "Go ahead. Knock on the door."

"I'll do it." JP walked toward the house.

"She ain't home," Gunner bellowed.

JP knocked on the door, pretty certain if Mrs. Holloway was in there, she wouldn't answer. He was right. He knocked again. Still nothing.

JP walked back to the truck, and DuBois nodded toward his car. JP turned in that direction, as did DuBois.

"This isn't over, Holloway," DuBois called out as he walked away.

"Don't come back without a warrant."

Behind the wheel, DuBois mumbled, "Like he's calling the shots."

"What now?" JP asked.

"I'm headed back to the department to see what I can find out about our canyon corpse, and you need to do whatever it is you do to find more suspects."

Chapter 13

Monday afternoon

Back at Sabre's office, JP continued researching her cases looking for any possible suspects. There were many possibilities, but few seemed likely. He hated this and wanted to do something productive. JP got up and paced the floor. *I can't just hang around here waiting for something to happen.* He grabbed his hat and looked at his watch. It was a two-hour drive to Pasadena, but he had to check out Lynch. The man was the only lead he had for now.

The drive was long and boring, but fortunately, the traffic wasn't too bad. As he made the last turn onto Lynch's street, his phone rang. The number from his home phone popped up on the navigation system. He pushed the button to connect his cell, proud of himself that it worked. He had just learned to work the system and wasn't sure he liked being so connected to the world, but this call was from home. "Hello."

"Hi, Uncle Johnny," Morgan said softly.

"Why are you whispering? Is everything okay?"

"Yeah, but I don't want Sabre to hear."

"Why not?"

"Because of the surprise, silly."

"What surprise?" JP asked.

"Uncle Johnny, are you okay?"

"Fine as a fiddle."

"Are you almost home? We have a lot to do before the party."

Oh no! Sabre's birthday party.

"I'm sorry, Munchkin. I'm working on a case, and I won't be home for a while." He heard her sigh with disappointment. "Don't worry. I'll call Ron, and he can pick up the cake and the balloons you wanted. Maybe you can go with him and get whatever you need."

"That would make Sabre suspicious."

"Ron's clever. He'll think of a good excuse."

"Will you be here for the party?" She sounded sad.

"I'll try my best. So let me get my work done."

JP hung up, called Ron, and asked him to take over. He gave him the name of the bakery and the flower shop. At least he'd had the good sense to order the gladiolas ahead of time. They were difficult to get this late in the season, and they didn't always have the color she wanted. Sabre liked them all, but the dark pink ones were her favorite. The flower shop couldn't promise the color, but they guaranteed the bouquet. Now, he just had to get home in time to join the surprise part of her thirty-first birthday party.

He drove up the block and parked in front of Lynch's two-story house, a beautiful old brick home. He walked up the path and rang the bell, anxious but determined.

"What are you doing here?" Todd's mother scowled as she answered the door.

"I'd like to see your son. Is he home?"

"No, he's not. Not that it's any of your business."

"Do you know when he'll be back?"

"If I did, I wouldn't tell you." She slammed the door.

That didn't take long. At least there's that. JP walked to his car. Before he got in, he glanced around the yard and saw movement on the side of the house. A tow-headed boy stood near the corner, peeking around. He held his hands out and made a motion like he was driving a car, then pointed down the street. *Was he telling him to drive farther away or telling him to leave?* JP got in his truck and moved it three houses down and out of sight from Lynch's house. He checked the time. If he didn't get going, he would hit rush hour traffic.

A minute later, the boy walked up and tapped on his passenger window. JP rolled it down. "Do you want to get inside?"

The boy glanced around, then opened the door and got in.

"You remember me, right?" JP asked.

"Yes. You were always nice to me, to all of us." The kid fidgeted in his seat.

"Which one are you? Sorry, I can't remember your name."

"I'm Evan, the youngest."

"You've grown since you were in San Diego."

"I know, but I'm still too small."

Did he want to be bigger so he could protect himself?

"I heard the conversation with you and Mrs. Lynch," Evan said.

JP found it odd that he didn't call her *Grandma*, but maybe she didn't want that. She was an odd, cold duck. JP had to ask. "Do you always call her Mrs. Lynch?"

"I have to. She says it shows respect, and the last thing I want is her mad at me."

JP didn't know what to say.

Evan went on. "She will never tell you anything about my dad. She hates you as much as he does."

"Yeah, I get that feeling." JP smiled. "Do you know where your father is?"

"He went camping."

"And he didn't take you boys with him?"

"No, we have school, but I don't like to go anyway. Nolan wanted to go, but Dad said no, and Nolan was pretty upset."

"When did your dad leave?"

"Friday sometime. He was already gone when I got home from school."

"Do you know when he'll be back?" JP asked.

The kid shook his head. "He didn't say."

"Do you know where he's camping?"

"Not really," Evan said. "He likes to go to the desert and use his Razor, but I don't know where."

"Have you ever been on the dirt bike?"

"Yes, but it scares me. Dad takes too many chances. He says it's perfectly safe, but I don't like it. Sometimes the rocks he goes over are really steep. I can't tell my dad that though because it makes him mad. Then he does it more, and I get more scared. Drew and Nolan both like it, though."

"Why are you telling me this?"

"Because you seem like a nice guy, and I really liked Ms. Brown. She tried real hard to keep us from going home with my dad."

"I'm sorry that didn't work out for you. Are you doing all right?"

"I guess. My mom's been clean for a while now. I'm hoping I can go live with her."

"What does your father think about that?"

"He doesn't know, and I won't tell him until I can do it. He'd kill me." The boy quickly added, "He wouldn't actually kill me, but he would be pretty mad. Every time one of us says anything about Mom, he blames Ms. Brown." Evan opened the truck door. "I'd better go before my grandma notices I'm missing."

"Thanks, Evan. You've been a big help."

JP checked the time and sped off.

Chapter 14

Monday evening

"Who all will be here tonight?" Dené asked. She and Morgan had just started putting up decorations in the backyard.

"Sabre's best friend, Bob, and his family. They have a son close to our age. You'll like him. Ron, of course, and their mother and her boyfriend, Harley. We call her Grandma. You'll like her too. And she always brings us cool gifts. I think she does it mostly because she loves to shop so much."

"Anyone else?"

"I don't think so. It was going to be bigger, but with everything going on with Sabre, this is better."

"Who's making dinner?"

"Everyone is bringing a dish. You know, like a potluck. We're barbecuing steak and hamburgers, with Uncle Johnny doing the grilling. If he makes it back in time."

"Where is he?" Dené asked.

"He's working on a case. I hate when he has to work late, but I think it has something to do with Sabre's accident."

"What happened to her, anyway?"

"I don't know for sure. The grownups don't want to worry us. I know her car got smashed up, and she doesn't remember what happened. Uncle Johnny says that happens sometimes when you have a blow to the head or a traumatic experience. I just hope he gets back in time for the surprise."

The girls hung the lights, except where they couldn't reach, and Conner did those for them. The plastic tablecloths were on the tables Conner had set up, and a gorgeous bouquet of purple and white gladiolas sat in the middle of one of the tables. Ron came out to let them know that his mom, Beverly, and her boyfriend, Harley, had arrived.

"Come on," Morgan said. "Let's go say hello."

Dené followed her inside. Morgan hugged a thin woman with perfectly styled hair and said hello to her boyfriend, who held an armful of gifts. After introductions, Morgan heard Dené repeat their names as if she was trying to make sure she remembered them.

"Where's Conner?" Beverly asked.

"Here I am, Grandma B," Conner said as he came around the corner.

"Before everyone gets here, I have presents."

Ron shook his head. "You don't have to do that every time you see the kids, Mom."

"I had to get something for Sabre, and since I was shopping anyway, I thought, 'What the heck?'"

Beverly reached for a gift bag from Harley and handed it to Conner. He opened it and found a new video game, then hugged her and thanked her. The second bag, much bigger, was for Morgan. It contained a stuffed giraffe.

"Thanks, Grandma. I love it."

"Well, you can never have too many giraffes."

Beverly pivoted. "I didn't forget you, Dené. It may take me a while to get to know your tastes, but I thought you might like to have this by your bedside." She handed her a wrapped box.

"Thank you," Dené said, feeling both grateful and awkward. When she opened the box, her eyes filled with tears. She removed a silver-and-black picture frame with a photo of her mother. "It's beautiful," she said. Dené cleared her throat and fought back tears. Then she hugged Beverly, not holding on too long.

"Sabre and your father found the photo for me." Beverly smiled kindly. "I hope you don't mind, but you should have something to look at when you feel lonely. We all need that."

"It's perfect."

Beverly turned to Conner. "Will you please go to my car and get the food out of the trunk? I brought a couple of different things. You can put them in the kitchen or wherever you're putting the food."

When Conner came back, he had a middle-aged man and his son with him. Dené thought she recognized the boy. After Conner introduced them, she said, "I know you from school, don't I?"

"Yes, we have homeroom together," CJ said.

Bob, his dad, suddenly said, "Sabre's five minutes away. I can see her on the Find My app."

Morgan glanced out the window, and Ron said, "Don't worry. JP's not far away. I just spoke to him."

"He'd better hurry, or he'll miss the surprise," Morgan said. "And we'd better all go out back and be ready."

The group moved into the backyard, and Dené stayed close to Morgan. A few minutes later, Sabre and another woman walked outside.

"Happy Birthday!" everyone shouted.

Just then, JP stepped up and put his hand on Morgan's shoulder. Apparently, he'd come in through the side gate. "Happy Birthday, Sabre." He walked up and gave her a quick kiss.

After a while, JP went into the house to get more sodas, and there was a knock on the door. JP answered it, surprised to see Travis Blodgett, Dené's father. "How are you?"

Travis was one of Sabre's Aunt Goldie's five kids. The family was dysfunctional in many ways, but Travis was the closest to normal. He was a charming ladies' man, but a hard worker, who was far less conniving or self-centered than the rest.

"I'm good." Travis narrowed his eyes. "You look surprised. Is this a bad time? Sabre said I could drop off some things and maybe spend a few minutes with Dené."

"It's fine. Come in. It's Sabre's birthday, and we're having a little celebration."

"I can come back tomorrow."

"No, please come in." JP led him to the backyard.

Sabre spotted them and approached. "Travis, I'm sorry. I totally spaced out that you were coming. I didn't know about the party, but you're more than welcome to join us. It'll give you a chance to see Dené in a casual setting."

"I don't want to intrude," Travis said.

"Don't be silly. You're family."

Beverly walked over, and Sabre said, "This is my mother, your Aunt Beverly. You may remember her."

"Aunt Bev, it's nice to see you again."

"You certainly have grown up," Beverly said. "And that daughter of yours is quite the young lady."

"I can't take credit for that, but thank you."

"Well, you certainly played a part in her looks. She's a beautiful young woman."

"Thank you." Travis seemed uncomfortable with the compliment and turned to Sabre. "Where is Dené?"

"She and Morgan are in their room. Let's go get her."

Sabre led Travis down the hall. The bedroom door was open, and the girls were sitting on the bed talking.

"Hi, Dené," Travis stepped into the room.

"Hi, Travis."

They chatted for a few minutes, both appearing uncomfortable, but Travis seemed to put everything he had into it. He struggled but kept the conversation going. "I brought your bike and helmet and a few other things I thought you might want right away. I have the rest of your belongings at my house. You and Sabre can come over and see what else you need."

"Thanks," Dené said. "It'll be great having my bike here."

"Let's go get it."

After they'd transferred her things, Travis and Dené joined the backyard crowd. Sabre watched Travis mingle with the crowd, talking mostly to Ron, but showing enough attention to Dené that she didn't feel slighted. Dené, on the other hand, seemed distant and quiet and pulled away from Travis every chance she got.

He only stayed an hour and left shortly after they ate dinner. Sabre was pleased with Travis' effort to get to know his daughter and thought the two might soon be a family. But as soon as he left, Sabre heard Dené say to Morgan in an angry voice, "Why didn't you tell me *he* was coming?"

Chapter 15

tuesday morning

The Eddie Blane Case

Sabre walked into a room at Rady's Children's Hospital where seven-year-old Eddie Blane slept, looking thin and frail. She pulled up a chair and sat, waiting for him to wake up.

About ten minutes later, a nurse came, woke him gently, and took his temperature.

"What is it?" Sabre asked.

"Normal." the nurse walked back out.

"Hi, Eddie," Sabre said.

"Who are you?"

She carefully explained her role in the court process, trying not to alarm him.

"Where's my mom?"

"I'm not sure. She may be working."

"When is she coming to see me? I miss her."

"She'll be here soon."

"Today?" His eyes opened wider with a glint of hope.

"I'm not sure. I'll see what I can find out. How are you feeling today?" Sabre asked.

"I'm okay. Can I go home?"

"You can't leave the hospital until your doctor says it's okay, and I'm not sure where you will go from here. We have to get you better before you can go anywhere." Sabre realized she hadn't answered his question, but she didn't want to disillusion him. Even if he wasn't really sick, his mental state was important.

In an attempt to talk about anything except his health, Sabre asked, "What do you like to do when you're not in the hospital?"

"I play video games."

"Do you do anything outside?"

"Not much." Eddie tried to sit up a little. "I want to learn to ride a bike, but Mom is afraid I might get hurt."

"Do you go to school?"

"I did once, but that was kindergarten. I kept getting sick, so Mom started home-schooling me."

"Do you have friends in your neighborhood you play with?"

"Not really. They have germs."

"All of them?"

"I used to have play dates," Eddie said. "But Mom stopped them because I always got sick after."

"What kind of symptoms do you get when you're sick?"

"Headaches and my stomach hurts. Sometimes, I throw up. And I get really tired." Eddie looked toward the door. "When is my mom coming?"

"I'll step out and make a few phone calls to see if I can find out about your mom's visit. You can rest while I'm gone."

"Okay." Eddie shut his eyes, and Sabre left the room.

In the hall, she called the social worker.

"We have a supervised visit set up for Thursday at ten o'clock," the social worker explained. Sabre had never had a case with this woman, mostly because the caseworker was young and new on the job. "That's the earliest we could get the supervision set up."

"Have you seen the mother and child together?"

"No, not yet."

"I'd like to supervise a visit so I can see how they interact," Sabre said. "Do you mind if I work with the mother's attorney to get her here? I won't let them out of my sight." When the woman hesitated, Sabre said, "If you need direction, please check with your supervisor. I know Maxine will approve it. The other option is for me to put the case on calendar tomorrow morning and ask the court to order it. Judge Hekman will not be happy that we're using court time, but she *will* order the visit, unless you have a profound reason not to allow it."

"I've never had this request before. I'll talk to my supervisor and let you know."

"Good idea. Can you do it right now while I'm on the phone?"

"I'll call you back."

Sabre went to the restroom and on her way back, her phone rang. It was Maxine Quinn. Sabre had worked many cases with Maxine before she'd become a supervisor. It was a well-deserved promotion, but Sabre hated to see her leave the trenches. She was so caring and efficient.

"Of course, you can set up the visit and supervise it," Maxine said. "Oaklyn is new, but she's diligent. Once she gets a little experience under her belt, she'll be a force to be reckoned with. Give her a chance, and if you have any other concerns, please feel free to call."

"Thanks. Eddie keeps asking for his mother, and considering the nature of the case, I'd really like to observe them together. I'll make sure she doesn't say or do anything that might affect his health."

"I trust you."

Sabre hung up, called Bob, and explained the situation.

"I'll check with the mother and see if she can go right now," Bob said. "Do you mind if I observe also?"

"Not at all. Just be sure to tell your client not to mention her child's health. We don't want her encouraging him to be sick."

~~~
~~~

When Bob walked into the room with Willow Blane, Eddie was sleeping again. He seemed to tire easily. *Was he really sick, or just not active enough to gain strength?*

Willow's eyes filled with tears when she saw the boy. "How's he doing?" she asked.

"He's tired, but no fever."

"I wish they could figure out what's wrong with him." She shook her head, sounding upset. "Everyone thinks it's me, but do you have any idea what it's like to see your son suffer every day and no one helps him?" Willow stared at Sabre. "I know you think it's my ..."

"Willow." Sabre cut her off. "I don't know enough about your child's medical history to form an opinion. I can assure you; I will do everything possible to get him the help he needs."

"Mom," Eddie said, opening his eyes, a faint smile on his face.

"Hi, love bug." She stroked his hair. "You're looking good today."

"When can I go home?"

"I'm not sure yet, sweetheart." Willow glanced at Bob, then at Sabre, as if looking for direction. Then she added, "You may have to go to another home for a while, but we're all doing everything we can to get you well so we can be together again."

Sabre was impressed. The mother was either genuine or very good at her cover up. Either way, it seemed to satisfy Eddie for the moment.

"I brought you your Game Boy so you would have something to do."

"Thanks, Mom. There's hardly anything on television."

"I know. Hopefully, this will help to pass the time." She squeezed his hand. "How are you feeling, baby?"

Eddie shrugged. "Not very good."

Sabre glanced at Bob, who, in turn, whispered something to his client. Willow changed the subject. They continued to visit with no more discussion about Eddie's health, and when the mother said goodbye, she held back her tears until she turned away and Eddie couldn't see them.

After the mother left, Bob walked Sabre to her car.

"I think that went pretty well, don't you?" Bob asked.

"They are definitely bonded." Sabre sighed.

"I know Willow had that one slip when she asked how he felt, but that's perfectly normal when someone is in the hospital."

"It's not that," Sabre said. "It was Eddie's response. When I asked him how he felt, he said, 'okay,' but he told his mother, 'not very good.' I'm not sure what it means. Maybe he thought he should be sick for her."

"Or maybe he was more comfortable telling his mother how he really felt," Bob countered. "Or maybe he felt better when you asked him. It may be nothing."

"Or it may be something."

Chapter 16

Chapter 16

Tuesday morning

JP slammed a file down on Sabre's desk. He really wanted to throw it across the room. He'd spent another two hours reading through files, but found nothing that might lead him to Sabre's attacker. Heck, he didn't even know if she had been assaulted. And it could be anyone from any one of her cases, or it could be none of them. If it was totally random, he had nowhere to start. He prayed that DuBois would come up with something soon. The only case he had to work with was the Waylon Holloway case. He checked his watch. He had an appointment to see Waylon in Urban Camp in forty-five minutes. It was only a fifteen-minute drive, but he wasn't making progress here, so he left.

In his truck, JP called DuBois. "Anything new?"

"Not yet. We still don't know who the dead man is."

"His identity would really help."

"On a hunch, I looked into another case," the detective said. "Five years ago, a man walked into a gay bar in Hillcrest and pummeled a guy. The victim went to the hospital with a broken jaw and a concussion. They never caught the assailant, but he fit the general description of Gunner Holloway."

"Was Gunner ever a suspect?"

"Not that I could tell. But get this, the victim was a teacher at the middle school where Waylon's brother attended."

"That's an interesting coincidence," JP said. "I'm on my way to see Waylon right now. If I get the chance, I'll find out what I can about the teacher."

"A witness said the perp came out of the bar and got in a truck with a kid who was about eleven or twelve. The witness didn't get a good look at either of them, so the age could be off."

"But you think that boy might have been Waylon?"

"It's possible."

~~~

JP walked into the interview room at Kearny Mesa Detention Center. He had never been to this part of the building. It was small, but had comfortable seating and art on the walls. So different from Camp Barrett or Del Campo, an old military barracks, where delinquents used to be housed. Waylon slouched on one of the sofas, looking a lot like his dad.

"Do you remember me?"

"Yes," Waylon said. "You're my lawyer's investigator, the Texan."

"That's me."

"Did something happen on my case?"

"No, but something happened to Ms. Brown."

His eyebrows furrowed with what appeared to be concern. "Is she okay?"

"Yes, but someone tried to hurt her."

Waylon sat up. "Was it my dad?"

"Why would you ask that?"

"Because he hates her, and you're here asking me questions."

"Why does your father hate Sabre so much? She really fought for you, even got you a good deal. And when you didn't take it, she still kept you out of state prison."
~~~

"I know." The boy shook his head. "I should've taken the plea deal. Then, at least, I'd be home with my mom. Now there's no one to protect her."

"Protect her from whom?"

"My dad and my older brother, Porter. He's meaner than dad. Faron, the oldest, used to protect her, but he moved to Montana. I miss him."

"Tell me a little about Faron. What is he like?"

"He's a good man. He's working in a tire shop in Helena and saving his money to get a little ranch."

"When did he leave home?"

"Right after he graduated from high school. He said he couldn't live under that roof anymore. I wanted to go with him, but he couldn't take me. He and Dad got into a huge fight about his leaving. Faron begged Mom to go with him and take me and Porter along, but Dad got wind of it and kicked him out. Dad wouldn't even go to his graduation, and they haven't talked since."

"Do you hear from Faron?"

"He calls me sometimes. He would call the house when he knew Dad wouldn't be there. Mom used to beg him to come home, but he wouldn't."

"Waylon, did your dad abuse you?"

"He beat Faron the most, but I would get a whippin' if I didn't do exactly what he asked, or if I talked back. I learned pretty quick just to do what he said, whether it was right or wrong. After that, I mostly got it for trying to protect Mom."

"What about Porter? Did your dad beat him, too?"

"Yes, but not as much. He always liked Porter best, but that's because he's just like him."

"Do your parents come to see you here?"

"My mom visits every couple of weeks, but she has to sneak away. Dad hasn't been here at all, and I don't want to see him. If I hadn't been such a chicken, I would've listened to

Ms. Brown instead of my dad, and I wouldn't be stuck in this hole."

"That's quite a change of attitude," JP said. "What happened?"

"There's a counselor here, Charles, who's been helpful. I fought seeing him at first, but then Faron convinced me to give him a chance. The funny thing is, my counselor is black. Can you imagine? My dad would flip out if he knew I was getting help from a black man."

"Do you remember about five years ago, a teacher at Porter's school got beat up in a bar?"

Waylon dropped his head. "Kind of."

JP decided to come right out and ask. "The attacker had a young boy, around eleven or twelve, with him. Was that you and your father?"

"No, but it might have been Porter. I don't know for sure, but there was a lot of whispering around the house when that happened, and Porter bragged about having a secret with Dad. The next year, I got that teacher for one of my classes, and my dad made my mom go to the school and get it changed."

~~~

JP called DuBois on his way out to his truck. When the detective picked up, he said, "Just the man I wanted to talk to. We have a name for the body."
~~~

Chapter 17

Chapter 17

Tuesday early afternoon

Sabre and Bob were already seated at the Vietnamese restaurant when JP joined them.

"Is this the new *Pho's*?" JP asked.

"We're testing it," Sabre said. "Bob has to find a #124 that's comparable. If they don't have it, we'll move on."

Bob found the entrée he was looking for.

"So, they do have it?" JP asked.

"Many restaurants serve it, but I haven't found one yet that's as good as Pho's. Maybe today's the day."

After a server took their order, Sabre turned to JP. "You said you have information from DuBois. Did he arrest someone?"

"No, not that good. But he did ID the dead guy as Harold Jenkins. Does that name mean anything to either of you?"

Bob gave it some thought, then said, "No."

Sabre shook her head. "But I'll check my files."

"What's his story?" Bob asked.

"He's thirty-eight and was born in Hope, Arkansas. No criminal history. He lives with his cousin just off Euclid. DuBois is meeting with the cousin as we speak. He'll call me when he's done."

Their food arrived, and they ate mostly in silence. When Bob pushed away his plate, Sabre asked, "How do you rate it?"

"I'd give it a seven. It's pretty close, but the pork isn't quite the same. Better than some, though."

"Yeah," Sabre said. "You gave the last one a four."

JP's cell phone rang, and he answered it, putting DuBois on speaker so they all could hear.

"His cousin was pretty upset," DuBois said. "She called Harold a 'real decent guy' who was down on his luck financially, but getting things together. He worked at a gas station and was saving his money for a car. In the meantime, he'd never complained about taking the bus to work and wherever else he needed to go."

"Does she know what he was doing in Clairemont Mesa?" Sabre asked. "Was he visiting friends?"

"The cousin had no idea why he was there. She said Harold had a girlfriend. She hadn't met her and doesn't know where she lives, but it could be that area. Harold's work schedule was the opposite of hers, so they didn't see each other that much." DuBois' tone shifted. "And before you go barreling over to Angela Madison's house, I've already talked to the aunt. She knows nothing about Harold and doesn't remember seeing any black men on her street or in the complex. But it's an enormous property, so he could've been visiting someone on another street."

"We'll go talk to Angela," JP said.

"I thought you might," DuBois said. "When? I'd like to tag along. I would go by myself, but I think it's better if Sabre is with the girl. She may feel more comfortable talking, and..."

"... and not fantasize?" JP asked.

"Yeah, that's it."

"One sec." JP pulled the phone back and looked at Sabre. "You heard him; DuBois wants to question Angela about the dead man. He'd like you along."

"Okay," Sabre said. "Angela gets home from school just after two."

JP checked his watch. "We can meet you there in forty minutes, DuBois, but let's not show her the corpse photo."

"I'm way ahead of you," DuBois said. "I got a recent picture from the cousin. I'll text it to you." The detective ended the call.

On their way out to the parking lot, Sabre worked through the logistics. "I'll ride with JP, and he can take me back to the courthouse to pick up my car later." Sabre turned to Bob. "Thanks for the ride."

"See you tomorrow," Bob said.

JP and Sabre were halfway to Angela's house when he asked, "What's bothering you?"

"I'm okay." She didn't sound fine, even to herself.

"You've hardly said a word since we left the restaurant. Are you okay with questioning Angela again?"

"No. I mean yes. It's j... just that I'm so frustrated that I can't remember anything. How could I block out so many hours of my day?"

"The doctor explained that. It's as plain as a pig on a sofa that something traumatic happened to you, and your conscious mind doesn't want to remember it. That was evident from the way you were found. You were running away from something awful."

Sabre smiled to herself at the way JP explained things. "I understand that, but it's still irritating. I'm a professional. I deal with horrible behaviors every day. Why was this so different?"

"I don't know, but I promise you we'll find out."

~~~

In Jan Webb's living room, DuBois showed her the photo of Harold.

"I don't recognize him. Sorry."

"No problem. Will you tell Angela we're here, please?"

Angela came in wearing a loose shirt tucked into her pants, a patch over one eye, and a pirate hat. She raised a
~~~

plastic sword and said, "Aye, matey. Return the treasure, or you'll have to walk the plank."

"Nice outfit, matey," DuBois said. "But shouldn't you have a parrot?"

"Of course I do, but he's out flying around right now. He doesn't like to be stuck inside all day."

"You're a good pirate, Captain," DuBois said, "very observant. I know you keep an eye on the ships and the sea all around you. Maybe you could tell us if you've seen this man before."

"Sure." She nodded and stood up straight, holding her sword upright.

DuBois took out his phone and brought up a photo of Harold Jenkins. "Do you recognize this man?"

Angela glanced at the image, then went back into her stance, sword held high.

"Angela, in real life, not pretend," Sabre said. "It's important that we know if he's been in this area."

The girl put down her sword and studied the photo. "Yeah, I've seen him."

"When?" DuBois asked.

She shrugged. "Lots of times."

"When was the last time you saw him?"

"Last week maybe."

"Did you see him last Friday, the day Sabre came here before her accident?" DuBois' phone beeped, but he ignored it.

"I don't know," Angela said.

"Was this the man sitting on the rock?"

"It might've been. I couldn't see his face from my room, so I'm not sure. And I didn't watch him very long."

"But you've seen him close enough to recognize him now, right?" Sabre asked.

"Yes, but not from my room."

"Where did you see him?" Sabre pressed.

"I'll show you." Angela walked upstairs to an open area that was set up like a family room, with a sofa, TV, and bookshelf. She walked to the window, and they all followed. The view encompassed the home's small backyard, the street behind them that ended in a cul-de-sac, and a row of houses across the way.

"You saw him from this window?" Sabre asked.

"Yeah. He walks from the street, then by the rock. And there's a gate at the end of the street. You can't see it from here, but he must come through there. Then he walks that way." She pointed to her left. "Then I can't see him after that."

Sabre counted the houses she could see before he would've disappeared out of her vision. There were four. She noticed JP and DuBois doing the same thing. JP moved his head with the count, and DuBois actually pointed and moved his lips. They all had the same idea.

They thanked Angela for being a good pirate and left the house. DuBois' phone beeped again. This time, he looked at it.

"I've got to go." He stopped. "And McCloud, I know you plan to canvas the area and look for Harold's girlfriend. Just don't mess anything up and let me know if you find her."

"Aye, Aye, Captain."

Chapter 18

Chapter 18

Tuesday afternoon

"I can take you back to your car and do this alone," JP said when they were outside.

"No, I want to help." Sabre walked toward the corner of the house. "I'll let you know if I get tired. We can cover a lot more ground with two of us."

JP agreed. "There's the gate." They squeezed through the partially open gate and walked toward the street ahead, which was two blocks long.

"Wow," Sabre said. "There are a lot more houses and condos back here than I imagined."

"And there's at least one more street that he could have been headed toward." JP pointed to pavement that led to another set of homes. "That one looks like it has units on both sides. But we can skip the first four here."

"How do you want to do this?"

"You take house number five. I'll do the next one, and we'll keep going until we reach the end or you want to stop. If we have to check the next street, we can each take a side."

Sabre agreed, knowing he didn't want her too far out of his sight.

Sabre's first stop was a family of four, and no one recognized Harold. Sabre used her phone to make a note of the address and the interaction. She saw JP take out his little notepad and takes notes at his house. They continued to the end of the street. Sabre was tired. Her injured feet hurt, but she didn't want to stop. She was too angry at herself for not remembering. They wouldn't be going through all this if she knew what actually happened.

"Why don't I go get the car and take you home," JP suggested. "I can finish later."

"No, let's keep going. If you have to come back, it'll be dark. Women living alone might not open the door to a strange man."

"Is that what you do after dark? Not answer your door, I mean."

"I don't answer to a strange man even during the day."

JP looked a little relieved.

"Which is all the more reason I should do this with you. Besides, people are getting home from work, so we won't have as many non-responses."

They rounded the corner, and JP crossed the street. When JP reached the third house, a woman opened the door and started shouting. Sabre was directly across from him and heard every word.

"I don't want what you're selling!" the woman bellowed. "If it's cable or phone service, I have what I need. If it's insurance, I got that too. If you're from the government, I won't help fund your corruption. If it's religion, I don't need any. Just go away and leave me alone." The door slammed. JP looked over at Sabre, raised both his palms as if to say, "Whatever," then walked on, shaking his head.

When Sabre reached the fifth house on her side, a short, black woman with gray hair and glasses answered the door.

"What can I do for you, young lady?"

"I'm an attorney at juvenile court, and I'm trying to find anyone who knows this man." She held her phone up so the woman could see.

"Is he okay?" the woman asked with concern.

"You know him?"

"Yes, Harold is a good man."

Sabre knew she had to tell her Harold was dead, but she couldn't get herself to say the words. "Did you happen to see him on Friday?"

"No, he was supposed to come here, but he never showed up. I've tried to call him a few times, but it goes right to voicemail. I figured he couldn't pay his phone bill again." The woman studied Sabre's face. "I can tell you're hiding something unpleasant. What is it? Did something happen to Harold?"

"I'm afraid so, ma'am."

"Is he… is he dead?"

"Yes," Sabre said, thinking she hadn't handled it well. "I'm so sorry."

The woman let tears roll down her cheeks. "He was such a gentle soul. What happened?"

Dang! Now what do I say? Sabre's frustration hit a new level. She didn't know if Harold Jenkins was her assailant or if he'd had anything to do with her. *Why can't I remember?* "My name is Sabre Brown, by the way."

"Velma Washington." Her voice went calm and sympathetic, easing Sabre's concern. "Now, honey, tell me what happened to Harold."

"We don't know exactly. He was found in the canyon, and he looked like he'd been beaten."

"Oh no. Who would do that? Harold wouldn't hurt anyone. I just know he wouldn't."

"Did you know him well?"

"I met him nearly forty years ago, but I've only *known* him a short time." She hesitated. "About three months ago, we sat next to each other on the bus. We got to talking and discovered we were both from Hope, Arkansas. He commented that the town was misnamed, and we both laughed about it. Come to find out, I knew him when he was just a little boy and went to school with his daddy. His mother was quite a bit younger. Oh, his daddy was such a handsome man. I had a crush on him, just like every other girl in town. His daddy knew how charming he was, and Harold was the result of one of his conquests. He didn't marry the girl, and he didn't stick around long after the baby was born. Harold was only two when his daddy left Hope and never returned. I left shortly after."

"So, you kept in contact with Harold after the bus meeting."

"My stop is at the bottom of that long hill you drove up to get here. When Harold realized that, he got off with me and carried my bags up here. He started coming back every week and fixing things around the house. He's been a godsend." She choked up. "I just don't understand why anyone would want to hurt him."

"We're trying to find out what happened."

Velma peeked around Sabre to look behind her. "Is that man with you?" She pointed at JP.

"Yes, that's my investigator." Sabre waved him over. "I want you to meet him. He may have to come back and ask more questions."

JP walked up, and Sabre made the introductions, then gave JP a quick synopsis of what Velma had said.

"We know Harold was living with a cousin in Encanto," JP said. "Did you ever meet her?"

"No. He spoke about her once, but he was quiet about his personal life. When we were together, he always wanted to talk about Arkansas."

"His cousin mentioned a girlfriend. Do you know anything about her?"

"That would be me." Velma laughed softly. "I wasn't his sweetheart, of course. That strapping young man wouldn't want an old woman like me. He was just teasing his cousin. She questioned where he went every Friday, and when he wouldn't tell her, she assumed he had a lady friend. He kept up the pretext because it drove her crazy. That don't mean he didn't have someone, but I think she was probably referring to me."

"I hate to ask this about your friend," JP said. "But did you ever see him display anger?"

"No, never."

"What about evidence of alcohol or drug use?"

"No, I never saw anything but a caring man."

Sabre thanked her for her time. JP left his card and asked her to call if she remembered anything that might help. "Detective DuBois is the lead on this case, so he'll probably be contacting you real soon. Please tell him anything you know that might help find Harold's killer." They walked away.

"At least we know why Harold was in the neighborhood," JP said.

"But we don't know why he was killed," Sabre countered. "Or why he was in the canyon, or if I'm the one who killed him, or if he's the guy I was running from. Dang! I've got to remember what happened. That's the only way to know anything for sure." She sighed. "What if I never remember?"

"Then we'll figure it out some other way."

In the truck, JP called DuBois, put him on speaker, and gave him Velma's address and a summary of their conversation. Sabre filled in a few details.

"You might like to know," DuBois said, "We found Harold's fingerprints on Sabre's car."

"Inside or out?" JP asked.

"Just the exterior on the passenger side. It doesn't appear he was ever inside the car."

"Is Sabre still a suspect?"

"Not in my mind."

Relief washed over Sabre.

DuBois continued, speaking directly to her. "You had some of the victim's blood on you. There's also evidence that a third person was at the scene. Most likely another man, and he's probably the killer. What we don't know is whether Harold and the other person were working together and something went wrong, or if Harold became a victim because he tried to help Sabre. There's any number of possible scenarios."

Chapter 19

Wednesday morning

The kids were still in bed, so JP and Sabre sat on the back patio drinking coffee. A mourning dove cooed, breaking the silence.

"Are you doing okay?" JP asked.

"I think so." Sabre paused. "My feet ache, and I keep bumping my scrapes so they hurt. I still can't remember a thing about what happened to me. We just took in a third child, and I have a case where it appears the mother has made her child so sick he can't live a normal life, and all he wants is to be with his mother. So, yeah, I'm good."

"I'm sorry, sweetheart."

"Thank you, but don't do that."

"Do what?"

"Try to take it all on your shoulders. I know this is just as hard on you. Morgan and Dené are not getting along as well as I hoped, and I know that makes you uneasy. What if the girls can't learn to get along?"

"They will. They just need to find some common ground."

"And then there's your brother. Gene won't be out of prison for a while yet and even when he is, it's hard to say if he'll settle down."

"That's a tough one. I know he'll want his kids, but I'm not handing them over that easily. The kids are getting used to having stability. So, he's going to have to prove himself."

"I agree, but with another teenager in the mix, we all have an adjustment to make. And who knows how much Dené's father will be involved. He's saying all the right things, but I don't know Travis that well, and his reputation isn't all that great. What if we end up having to raise them until they're adults?"

He put his hand on her knee and looked at her lovingly. "Then that's what we'll do."

"I know. And I know losing my memory is frustrating for you as well. You want my memory to come back as much as I do."

"What's your point?"

"You don't have to try to take it all on your shoulders. We're in this together."

"It's just that I have no idea what to do next," JP said. "It's like all I can do is send things up the flagpole and see who salutes."

Sabre laughed. "Yeah, that's exactly the way I would've put it."

"It's nice to hear you laugh."

"You do that for me. Know what else you can do for me?"

JP grinned.

"No, not that. I need you to investigate the Eddie Blane case, the alleged Munchausen issue."

"What's your take on it?" JP asked.

"I'm trying to keep an open mind, but this kid has had many hospital stays and trips to the doctor, and the medical professionals still can't figure out what's wrong with him. He's tired all the time, sick to his stomach, gets dizzy, and he's in pain. And the mother gets lots of attention for her child's maladies. She's always posting about it on Facebook, and she has a whole blog dedicated to it. She has thousands of followers on her blog."

"How can someone make their kid sick just for attention?" JP hissed.

"We don't know for sure that's what's happening."

JP shook his head, his face tight with frustration.

"You seem pretty upset," Sabre said. "Can you be open-minded when you investigate this case? I really need to know the truth for this kid's sake."

"I'll treat it like all your cases, especially your delinquents. If I assume they're guilty, that's all I seem to find. But if I assume they're innocent, I turn up everything, which usually proves they're guilty, because most of them are, but when they're not, I'm pleasantly surprised." He grinned. "So, what do you want me to do?"

"I'm hoping to get a CASA worker on the case, maybe someone with medical training. So, for now, you don't need to talk to any medical professionals. That might come later. But I want you to question neighbors, family, school employees, anyone who knows them personally. Also, see if there is a relative for possible placement. Do you have time for all that?"

"I'm on it. But if DuBois calls and needs me for your case, I'll switch back."

"I know where your priorities lie."

Noise emanated from the kitchen. "Our quiet time is over," Sabre said. She and JP both stood and went inside. "I made a copy of the Blane file for you. It's on the desk."

Morgan, Conner, and Dené were all in the kitchen. Morgan and Dené each had a bowl of cereal, but sat at opposite ends of the table. Sabre looked at each of them and then at Conner.

"They're not talking this morning." He gulped down his orange juice. "I'm off. See you later."

Sabre sat down. "Do you two want to tell me what's wrong?"

"She started it," Morgan said.

"That's not true," Dené snapped.

"Forget who started it. What's the problem?"

"Nothin'." Dené picked up her bowl and took it to the sink. She noisily rinsed it out and put it in the dishwasher, then headed toward her room.

"We'll talk about this later," Sabre said.

Chapter 20

Wednesday morning

The Eddie Blane Case

After studying the file, scheduling appointments, and setting up a route to visit his interview subjects, JP began his sojourn around the community.

His first stop was the Blanes' next-door neighbor, Isabelle Zeller, a short, gray-haired woman. She greeted JP with a smile and invited him inside. It always surprised him when strangers did that. *How does she know I'm not dangerous?* Isabelle moved swiftly despite the extra weight she carried.

JP sat in the chair she offered him. "How well do you know Willow Blane?"

"She's lived next door for about two years, and I see her a lot. So, pretty well."

"Would you say you're friends?"

"We don't socialize out of the neighborhood." She straightened her glasses. "So, I'd say really good neighbors more than friends."

"What is she like?"

"She's very friendly, a little obsessed with her son, but that makes sense because of his health."

"I take it you know Eddie?"

"Yes. I've seen him when I've visited Willow." She adjusted her glasses again. "He doesn't go outside much. Occasionally,

I've seen him in the backyard, but not often. He's very sick, you know."

"I understand that," JP said. "Have you seen him when he's sick?"

"He's always sick, in and out of the hospital all the time. I feel so sorry for both of them. I heard CPS took him away from her."

"Where did you hear that?"

"Willow told me. She's very upset." Once again with the glasses. "She wrote about it in her blog, but I guess she needed someone to talk to in person."

"Did she tell you why they took him away?"

"She said they think she's making him ill. That's crazy. Why would a mother make her own kid sick? She loves him very much. She's never mean to him. In fact, she has more patience than any parent I've ever seen. She wears herself out trying to take care of that sick boy, and they treat her like that. I think it's just awful."

Everyone has an opinion. All I want is some facts. JP couldn't fathom the idea that a parent could intentionally make his or her child ill just for the attention. But then he thought about all the horrible things parents do to their kids and this was not even close to the worst.

JP interviewed three other neighbors with virtually the same result. Willow was a lovely lady with nothing but concern for her son. They all knew about CPS involvement, so she couldn't have wasted any time telling the neighborhood.

Her sister, Klara, had a little different take on the situation. Like the others, she knew what was going on. JP had to admit it made his investigation easier. Usually, witnesses didn't know about the juvenile court case, and because it was all confidential, he had to be careful with his questioning. Willow, on the other hand, had told the world what had happened.

"Do you see your sister much?" They stood in her kitchen while they talked.

"Not a lot. She's always so busy with her *sick* son."

JP couldn't help but notice the emphasis. "You make it sound like Eddie might not be sick. Do you think there's something else going on?"

"I don't know." She sighed. "I think it's about time CPS got involved. There is something seriously wrong in that house. If he's really as sick as she claims, the doctors need to find out what is wrong." Klara hesitated. "And if he isn't sick, then Willow needs real help." She flung her long, straight hair over her shoulder, and JP noticed the resemblance to her sister.

"Do you spend any time with Eddie?"

"I used to have him over once in a while, but the older he got, the sicker he got, and the less she'd let him stay with me."

"Has he been sick since he was born?"

"He was sensitive to a lot of things as a baby and toddler. Willow was always over-protective of him. She feared he might catch something, but he seemed healthy for the first couple of years, except for some allergies. She kept him in a bubble even then, but he developed asthma by the time he was three." She paused again, as if she didn't want to tell everything.

"Klara," JP said softly. "I really need to know everything. Eddie's attorney wants to help him, and she'll do everything she can to protect him."

"Things got worse after her husband left. That's when Eddie started getting sick all the time. I don't know if this Munchausen thing is true or not, but I know my sister gets a lot of attention out of it. I hate to think bad about her, but I feel so sorry for Eddie. If she is making him sick, she has to stop."

"Eddie can't go home with Willow when he leaves the hospital. Is there any chance you'd be willing to take him for a while?"

"The social worker asked me the same thing. At first, I didn't want to because it would mean dealing with Willow all the time, but the more I think about it, the more I want to help Eddie. And if he's here for a while and gets better, that would be great. And if he doesn't, then maybe it's not Willow's fault."

"Have you told the social worker you may be willing to take him?"

"Not yet, but I'll call her when you leave. I heard Eddie might be released today, and she said if I was interested, they'd have to evaluate my home."

"Do you mind showing me around so I can report back to Eddie's attorney?"

"Of course."

The house was a clean, three-bedroom in Mission Hills with impeccable furnishings. Klara worked from home doing medical billing on a contract basis. For the last eight years, she'd also helped her husband with his realtor business. Their garage housed a new Toyota Camry and an old Porsche.

As JP walked out, a man in a two-year-old Mercedes pulled into the drive. He stepped out of the car and offered his hand. "I'm Jon, Klara's husband. Nice to meet you. Klara said you were coming by."

"Nice to meet you as well." JP shook his hand.

"We're thrilled social services finally got involved. It should've happened long ago. That poor kid has suffered all his life."

"Because of his illnesses?"

Jon tipped his head. "Because of his mother. Klara doesn't really want to see it, but that boy is always sickest when he's with his mom. Willow has always been jealous of her sister, and when Eddie was born, she found a way to keep the attention on herself."

"So, you don't think Eddie is really sick?"

"Oh, he's sick all right, because his mother makes him sick. He does have asthma, but I'm not even sure how bad that is. We've tried to get her to let him stay with us for a week and see how he does, but she'd never leave him for more than a couple of hours. Willow is the sick one."

Chapter 21

Chapter 21

Wednesday morning

JP entered the portable trailer on the construction site in East County where Porter Holloway worked. A man was talking on his cell phone, then hung up and asked, "What can I do for you?"

"I understand you have a young man named Porter Holloway working for you. Is that correct?"

"Yes. Is he in trouble?"

"Not that I know of," JP said. "Why would you ask?"

"No reason," the man said. "What do you want?"

"I'm JP Torn, a private investigator. I'm following up on a case."

"So, Porter is in trouble? I hope it's not serious. He's a bit of a hothead, but he's a good worker. He's still in the honeymoon stage, so that might wear off though. What did he do?"

"Actually, it's his brother's case, but I'd like to ask Porter some questions."

"He's putting up drywall in the third house down."

JP started to leave, then turned back. "How long has he worked for you?"

"About three months. He doesn't have much experience, but he's strong as a bull, not afraid to get dirty, and really wants to learn construction."

"You said he was a hothead. What did you mean by that?"

"He's opinionated and ready to fight at the drop of a hat. I didn't like his attitude when he applied for the job, but I needed the help, so I gave him a chance."

"Thanks," JP said and stepped toward the door. "Do you know what time Porter left work last Friday?"

"We all took off around three."

JP nodded and walked out.

Several men were working in the house, but based on the "strong as a bull" description, Porter was easy to pick out. Even though he was shorter than his brother, his well-developed biceps bulged with tattoos, and his leg muscles bulged through his tight jeans. He wasn't as attractive as Waylon, and from everything JP had learned about him, he wasn't as pleasant or likable as either of the other boys. In that respect, he truly favored his father.

"Porter Holloway?" JP asked, as he walked up to the man hanging drywall.

"In the flesh," Porter said. "Who wants to know?"

"JP Torn. I'm a private investigator."

"I ain't done nothin'." He set down a heavy piece of drywall.

"I work for the attorney who represents your brother, Waylon."

"His case is over. Haven't you heard? He's servin' time."

"Something has come up that we're investigating."

Porter shook his head and made a *tsk* sound. "What's that wuss done now?"

"It's not that. Can you tell me what time you left work on Friday?"

"It was late, maybe seven, but what business is that of yours?"

That didn't match what his boss had said. JP ignored it for now. "Have you seen your brother since he's been in custody?"

"No. We don't get along that well."

"Why's that?"

"Because he's an idiot and a wuss."

"That's the second time you've called him that. Why?"

"Look, the kid's a pansy. I'm always having to fight his battles for him. The one time I make him stand up for himself, he gets arrested and blames me for his trouble."

"You made him stand up for himself when he beat that young man?" JP asked.

"I told him if the kid bothered him, do something about it."

"Was the kid bothering him?"

"Look, we don't have to put up with guys like that. The Bible says so."

"I don't think there's anywhere in the Bible that encourages you to hurt other people."

"What do you want?" Porter snapped.

"About five years ago, were you with your father when he beat up the schoolteacher at the bar?"

He smirked. "I don't know what you're talking about."

He obviously wasn't going to tell on his father, but his demeanor said it all. JP moved on. "Did you see your father on Friday?"

"Why don't you ask him?" Porter smirked. "Oh, that's right, you can't. He's gone."

"Where did he go?"

"Not that it's any of your business, but my mother caught him with a younger woman. They had a big fight, and he left."

"Is your mother okay?"

"She's fine. Like my dad says, if she would lose some weight, he wouldn't have had to go lookin' elsewhere for someone sexy."

"And you think that's okay?"

"I don't make the rules."

JP wanted to punch him. He was even more irritating than his father. "Where did your dad go?"

"I don't know."

"Have you heard from him?" JP asked.

"That's none of yer business."

"Did he beat your mother up before he left?"

"That's it. I'm done talkin'. I'm not gonna narc on my father. You're not a cop, and I'm done talkin' to you." He turned and started his drill to shut down the conversation.

JP watched him drill into drywall for a moment, then left and called DuBois.

"I just questioned Porter Holloway. He's got a burr in his saddle, just like his father. He said his parents had a fight and Gunner left. And he claims he left work on Friday around seven in the evening, but his boss said everyone left about three. He also thinks the only thing Waylon has ever done right in his life is beat up that innocent kid."

"Sounds like a real winner."

"You have no idea," JP said. "But with the guard dog gone, we can probably talk to Gunner's wife."

"I'll meet you there."

Chapter 22

Chapter 22

Wednesday morning

"Do you mind if I take the lead on this?" JP asked as he and DuBois stepped onto the front porch of the Holloway trailer.

"Feel free, McCloud," DuBois said. "You know the Holloways better than I do, and you've already spoken to Waylon and Porter. Besides, you'd probably do it anyway."

It took three knocks on the trailer door before Mrs. Holloway answered. "He's not here," she said. "He left."

"We heard." DuBois eased forward. "We're here to see you. Can we come in? We won't take much of your time."

"I've got plenty of time." She pushed the door open wider and stepped back.

JP got a good look at the bruise on the side of her face.

"Come in. Have a seat," the battered woman said.

The doublewide was clean and well kept. The inside looked much better than the outside.

"Are you okay?" JP asked.

She reached up and touched her cheek. "Oh, this? I got off easy this time." She lowered her eyes. "I usually can't leave the house for weeks after Gunner spirals. The physical abuse doesn't hurt nearly as much as the horrible things he says to me." Her eyes tightened with emotional pain. "He used to apologize. He doesn't even do that anymore. He was never sorry anyway, so I guess it doesn't matter. But you didn't come here for that. What do you want to know?"

"Let's start with last Friday," JP said. "Was Gunner home with you like he said?"

"No." She stared at her hands in her lap. "He came home from work about three o'clock, took a shower, and went back out. All he said was not to wait up, not a word about where he was going. He came home about two in the morning."

"And you have no idea where he went?"

"I have an idea. I'm just not sure which woman."

"Was that a regular Friday night occurrence?"

"It wasn't unusual that he went out, but it was odd that he went that early. Normally, he eats dinner and leaves about eight. He used to say he was going out drinking with the guys. Lately, he didn't bother with any pretense."

JP hated wife beaters and child abusers. Gunner seemed to be both. And he might have been responsible for the violence on Sabre. "Did he ever talk about Waylon's court case?" JP asked.

"He was mad at Waylon and yelled at him a lot for it."

"Angry because Waylon beat up the kid?"

"No," she scoffed. "Because he got caught. Or didn't finish the job. You pick."

"Did he ever say anything about Waylon's attorney?"

"For starters, he didn't want a woman lawyer. He swore she'd lose the case because she was incompetent. As I'm sure you know, he doesn't think women are too smart."

"Yeah, I got that," JP said.

"I guess I haven't done much to prove otherwise."

JP wasn't sure how to respond to that, so he let it slide. "Did he ever make any threats toward Ms. Brown?"

"He threatened to kill her if she didn't win the case, but he was always threatening to kill someone, so I don't know if he really meant it." Mrs. Holloway looked directly at JP for the first time. "Did something happen to Ms. Brown?"

"I'm afraid so, but she'll be okay."

"I hope he didn't hurt her." The woman lowered her eyes again. "When is it going to stop?"

"You have to report his abuse," DuBois said. "I can pass your statement to the domestic violence unit, but it means you'll have to take a stand against him."

"I don't know if I'm that strong."

"But he's gone now, right?"

"Yes, but he's left before. Chances are he'll be back."

"Maybe not this time. Do you know where he is?"

"He left his job as a mechanic and started driving trucks across country. Or at least that's what Gunner told me. It wouldn't surprise me, though. He used to drive years ago. Those were the best years of our marriage. Probably because he was gone so much. I haven't heard from him since he left, and likely I won't until he decides to return." She went into the kitchen, came back with a business card, and handed it to DuBois. "Here's where he works. He's still at the same company, just in a different position now. They should be able to tell you where he actually is."

"What about Porter?" JP asked. "Was he home Friday night?"

"Do you think he had something to do with Ms. Brown's accident?"

"We're just trying to rule things out. Would he have any reason to hurt her?"

"I don't understand anything Porter does anymore. He was such a sweet boy, but I lost him to Gunner years ago. Porter looks up to him and emulates everything he does. So, to answer your question, I don't think he had a reason to hurt Ms. Brown, but he would do whatever his father told him to, and he'd do anything to look good in Gunner's eyes." She paused for a second, as if trying to recall something. "Porter came home after work, asked me to make him a sandwich while he showered, then left just after his father did."

So, why did Porter lie about leaving work so late on Friday?

Chapter 23

Chapter 23

Wednesday early afternoon

Sabre finished her morning calendar earlier than usual and returned home. She didn't feel like going back to her office so when JP called, she agreed to meet him at home. She needed to see what, if anything, he had discovered. Maybe he had found something that would help her remember.

She had only been home a short time when JP arrived. Sabre fixed some sandwiches and set them on the table.

"Are you hungry?" Sabre asked.

"I could eat." He took a soda out of the refrigerator and popped the top. Neither of them spoke for a few minutes.

Finally, Sabre asked, "So, what've we got?"

"Well, we haven't confirmed alibis for any of our suspects—Gunner, Porter, or Lynch. It could be any of them."

"Or none," Sabre said. "It could be Harold. We know he was there. Maybe he attacked me, I killed him, and then ran away. Maybe it's that simple."

"But DuBois said someone else was there, likely another man. And why would Harold attack you? Velma seems to think he's a nice guy."

"True, but we don't really know much about him. He could've been mental, or had a grudge against women, or needed money and saw a chance to get some. Who knows? Velma doesn't know him that well."

"I wish the case was as simple as your theory, but I think there's a lot more to it than that."

"Maybe that's because you want someone to suffer for hurting me, and since Harold is already gone, you need another suspect."

"Or maybe my gut is right, and it won't let me move on until we figure this out."

"It would be a lot easier if I could just remember what happened."

"Stop beating yourself up. Hopefully, something will trigger your memory, and it will all come back to you."

"That's it," Sabre said. "Let's go to the canyon where they found my car. Maybe I'll remember something."

"I'm not sure that's a good idea."

"Why not? This is driving me absolutely crazy. I spend more time thinking about what I can't remember than I do remembering what I did a minute ago. I'm in a fog and I hate it."

"Okay, let's go." They walked out to the truck and climbed in. JP sat in the driver's seat without starting the engine. "This may not work, you know?"

"Or it might."

JP started the vehicle and pulled out of the driveway.

When they reached the shopping center on Balboa, JP pointed to the front of the CVS drug store. "That's where the cops found you."

He turned into the parking lot and followed the route Sabre had taken. "We know you ran across this lot because of the witnesses."

Sabre studied the area, taking in the store facades, the pavement, the cars. Nothing triggered a memory.

When JP reached El Portal, he said, "This is where you entered the parking lot. A restaurant employee saw you run in. She wasn't sure which way you came from, but considering your shoe was found at Boyd and Genesee, we think you came from the south. DuBois has been canvassing the area to see if anyone saw you, but there's a lot to cover. I told him I'd help later today. Right now, he's more concerned about what happened before you started your run." JP paused. "Is any of this helping?"

"It's all familiar, but I've been here before, several times. I don't think any of those memories are from Friday night."

From the parking lot, it was a short distance until they passed Angela's house, then turned into the opening to the canyon. JP stopped the truck as close to the scene as he could.

Once on foot, Sabre followed JP to where they had found her car.

He pointed to the tracks where the car had obviously been towed away. "Right there."

Sabre stepped closer until she was standing near a bush that still had a piece of crime-scene tape attached. She tried so hard to remember that it made her head hurt. She walked around, but nothing came to her. "Where was Harold found?"

JP took her to the exact spot. Sabre looked closely at the rocks, the ground, the brush. *Were those dark spots Harold's blood?* Her head pounded, and her lungs felt tight.

"What's wrong?"

"I remember something." Sabre took a deep breath. "A man is trying to open the car door. I'm stuck in the car, and I'm hurting and afraid. He opens the driver's side and yanks me out."

"Do you recognize him?"

"No, I can't see his face."

"What happened next?" JP asked.

"It's all kind of blurry. I can see a black man, but I don't think he's the same man who pulled me out of the car. I'm just not sure."

"Do you think it's Harold?"

"I don't know."

"Anything else?"

Sabre closed her eyes tight, thinking about what she had just remembered and trying for more, or at least a clearer picture. But nothing. Her phone rang. "It's Maxine, probably with something on the Blane case." Sabre took the call and just listened. "I'll be right there. I'm only a few blocks from her house." She hung up. "Let's go."

"What is it?" JP asked.

"It's Angela. She's missing."

Chapter 24

Chapter 24

Wednesday afternoon

Sabre and JP arrived at Angela's house before anyone else. Sabre assumed Maxine had called the police, and she herself would be there shortly. JP called DuBois to update. Though they couldn't be certain, it seemed likely that Angela's disappearance was connected to Sabre's incident.

"What happened, Jan?" Sabre asked.

"I don't know. I took her to school this morning, but when I went to pick her up, she wasn't there." Sabre looked at the clock on the wall. Jan must've noticed because she said, "It was early dismissal today. They got out at one."

"Did you talk to anyone at school?"

"According to the principal, she never went to class at all."

"Have you called her friends?"

"Yes, she has two really good friends. One goes to private school and lives up the street. She hasn't seen or talked to Angela today. The other, Yvette, said she wasn't at school. She didn't see her at all."

"When you dropped her off, did you walk her inside the building?" Sabre asked.

"No, but I watched her until she went inside."

The doorbell rang, and Jan answered it. A police officer came in. Jan made the introductions, then repeated what she had just told Sabre and JP.

"Has she ever done this before?" the cop asked.

"No, but she's such an adventurous kid. Not much scares her, and she fantasizes all the time about going places and doing things. That's why I watch her so closely."

The doorbell rang again. "I'll get it," Sabre said. This time it was Detective DuBois. Sabre greeted him, then explained what little she knew.

DuBois nodded at JP, said hello to Jan, then turned to the officer. "I'm Detective Vincent DuBois, and I'd like to finish the questioning, if you don't mind. I've previously met both the aunt and the missing child. We think this may be related to a homicide we're investigating."

"By all means."

"Did Angela say anything that might be construed as a plan to run away?" DuBois asked.

"No," Jan said.

"Has she mentioned any people she's seen or talked to lately?"

"No."

DuBois asked more questions about her behavior and actions, especially during the last twenty-four hours, but nothing seemed important.

Sabre stepped forward. "Do you mind if I ask a couple of questions?"

"No," DuBois said, "go ahead."

"When I was here on Sunday, Angela was pretending to be a pirate. Did she keep that up, or did she change characters?"

"She's been a pirate ever since last Thursday," Jan said, scowling. "Which is a little unusual. Normally, she changes characters daily. She often acts out a familiar character, but only for a day or two at a time. How does that matter?"

"When she watched *Anne, With an E*, on television, she became Anne. When she watched *Sabrina*, she acted like a witch. When she recovered from being sick, she became a nurse. When I first came onto this case, she played lawyer.

Angela acts out whatever is going on in her life. But if she's stuck on being a pirate, it might mean something." Sabre paused. "What does she talk about when she's in character?"

"You know Angela," the aunt said. "Half the time she doesn't make sense. And I tune her out a lot, because she talks non-stop." Jan fought back tears. "Do you think maybe she said something that might help us find her, and I wasn't listening?"

"I don't know," Sabre said. "Just tell us everything you remember."

"She's been using an Australian accent." Jan's brow furrowed as she tried to recall. "And Angela mentioned several times that the bad pirates want the treasure. She also keeps talking about making the bad guys walk the plank. I don't know how that helps. Most of what she says is gibberish."

"I'll give it some thought," Sabre said.

The police officer stepped forward. "We have to get out an alert, so I'll need a physical description and photo of Angela."

Sabre, JP, and DuBois moved a few steps away. "What do we do now?" Sabre asked.

"I know Jan talked to Angela's friends, but I'll question them again," DuBois said. "First, I'll stop by the school and see if anyone saw her after she was dropped off this morning."

"How can I help?" JP asked.

"We'll have plenty of manpower on Angela's case once we know where to start looking. If anything changes, I'll let you know and you can join forces with me. In the meantime, I haven't had time to trace Sabre's path last Friday, so if you could question residents between the canyon and the shopping center, maybe it will lead us to something. If these two cases are connected, it may help us find Angela."

Chapter 25

Chapter 25

Wednesday afternoon

When the officer left to talk to neighbors, DuBois and Jan went upstairs to search Angela's room. DuBois suggested Sabre go with them, in case they found something she thought was important. JP had already left to find more witnesses.

"You'll find lots of secret hiding places with little trinkets tucked away. She loves secret compartments," Jan said. "You wouldn't believe the things I've found while I was cleaning."

"Like what?" DuBois asked.

"I've found a few live creatures, like bugs in a jar. Angela always puts holes in the top so they can breathe. I've found coins she's picked up. She likes coins, especially foreign ones, and she saves ribbons and buttons. As you know, she likes to dress up and play make-believe, so I've taken her to thrift stores to find old jewelry and other stuff for costumes. I really have to control her, though. She wants to buy everything."

The officer continued to search the room, looking at boxes within boxes. Nothing seemed unusual, at least unusual for Angela. When they came across her box of pirate stuff, DuBois dumped it out on the bed and sifted through it. An eye patch, a pirate hat, some coins, and a cylinder-shaped piece of wood. He held up the dowel and asked, "Do you know what this is about?"

"That's a peg leg," Jan explained. "She ties it on her knee and walks around with it."

Then he opened a small cardboard box with the word *Treasure* written on it. Inside was a flash-drive keychain shaped like an airplane, with blue lettering on the side. "What's this?"

"It's just a trinket," Jan said.

"Why would a young girl have a flash drive?"

"I don't know. I thought it was just a cute keychain."

DuBois looked at Sabre.

"I've never seen it before," Sabre said.

"It seems strange that her old-time pirate treasure is a modern flash drive, doesn't it?"

"Maybe," Sabre said. "But there's also a skeleton key. Maybe she just wanted something to put the key on."

DuBois looked at Jan. "Do you know what the key is for?"

"No," Jan said. "It might be something she got from the thrift store or a garage sale. Sometimes, she picks up an entire box of things for a buck or two. I just buy them for her, because she has so much fun with all of it." Jan paused. "But if I remember right, it used to have two other keys as well."

"Do you know what they were for?"

"No. As I said, I just thought it was something random we bought."

"They weren't for your house?"

"No, they looked like house keys, but they were a different shape than mine."

DuBois bagged the treasure box and took it with him.

Chapter 26

Chapter 26

Wednesday late afternoon

With a photo of Angela loaded on his phone, JP canvassed the neighborhood. DuBois had given him a list of places they'd already covered, which included the houses on the hill. One woman had been in her backyard Friday evening and had seen someone running out of the canyon. The witness thought the runner looked like a woman, but she couldn't give a better description.

JP walked toward his truck and was about to get in when he saw Fishing Boy walk out of his house. JP checked the list DuBois had given him. That address wasn't on it. "Excuse me," JP called out as he approached the kid, who looked about twelve. "Do you know the young girl who lives in that house?" He pointed to Angela's.

"I've seen her around, but I've never talked to her."

"Have you seen her today?"

"No."

"Were you here on Friday afternoon or early evening?"

The kid shrugged. "I think I got home around four-thirty."

"Did you happen to see a man in a blue sweatshirt and jeans hanging around the common area over there?"

"You mean Harold?"

"You know him?"

"He comes here every week to help some old lady around the corner. He sits on the rock and smokes a cigarette beforehand. If I'm outside, he stops and talks to me. He always asks if I've caught any fish, and he tells stories about the fishing holes in Arkansas. He said some had so many fish, you could reach down and grab them with your hand. I think he was exaggerating, but it was a good story."

"And you saw him last Friday?"

"Yeah. When I came outside to mow the lawn, he waved. A few minutes later, he ran past me really fast."

"Which way did he go?"

The boy pointed in the direction of the canyon. "That way, down the hill."

"Did you see anyone else? Was he chasing someone, or was someone chasing him?"

"No, I don't think so."

"Did you see any cars?"

He shrugged again. "A few cars came and went, but nothing that seemed related to him running."

"Was one of those cars a green BMW?"

"Could have been. I didn't pay that much attention."

"Did you hear anything? Any shouting or talking?"

"No, but I had my earbuds in, and I was listening to music. I play it pretty loud, so I don't hear much." He looked closer at JP. "Are you a cop?"

JP was surprised at how much the boy had shared without asking who he was. But the kid was young and not overly suspicious yet. "No, I'm a private investigator. My name is JP Torn."

"I'm Luca." He seemed to study JP's expression. "Is Harold okay?"

"No." JP took a breath. "I'm afraid not."

He thanked Luca and left. Then he drove up the block and stopped at several more houses. No one had seen Angela or Sabre. Once he covered all the houses from which someone could've seen the area where she ran, he drove down the hill and turned off Boyd onto Genesee. Across the street from where the shoe had been found stood a block of condos. JP entered the complex from the backside, parked, and walked to the doors facing the street. He started on the top floor and tried three before he found anyone home. The owner wasn't there on Friday, so he was no help. Another person was home on Friday, but didn't see anything. Finally, he reached the corner condo directly across from the intersection.

A young man answered the door. JP explained who he was and asked if he'd been present Friday evening.

"No, but my roommate might be able to help you." He turned and yelled, "Quan."

Another young man, almost as tall as JP, came to the door. JP repeated his spiel. "Were you here Friday night?"

"Yeah, I was working on a paper that was due on Monday."

"Did you happen to see a woman running down the street?"

"I did. Is she all right?"

"She's fine, but someone else was hurt, and we're trying to find out what happened. Where was the woman when you saw her?"

"Come in. I'll show you." JP followed Quan into the small dining area. "I was sitting there." He pointed to a chair by the window, which gave him a perfect view of the street.

"What exactly did you see?"

"It was already getting dark, but a woman suddenly appeared under that streetlight, coming from the direction of the hill. She stopped for a second and looked around, then started running again toward Balboa. She was carrying her shoes and dropped one as she took off. I watched her until she went out of sight, which wasn't very far."

"Do you mind if I sit in the chair so I can see?"

"Go ahead, but I think I stood up and got closer to the window so I could see a little better."

"Okay, I'll do that." JP sat in the chair, then got up as Quan had, but it didn't change anything. "Did you see anyone else? Someone who might have been chasing her?"

"No."

"Did you see any vehicles come down the hill about that time?"

"I don't think so. I know the light was green because a car had just passed through it when I spotted her. Shortly after, another came from the other direction, but that's all I saw while she was there."

"And no one stopped?"

"No."

"Thank you, Quan. You've been a big help."

"I'm glad to know she's okay. It seemed so strange that a woman was out running after dark. I didn't think much of it until I saw she was barefoot. I thought about calling the police, but what would I say? I figured she was probably a homeless person, acting strange. Now, I feel bad for not doing anything."

"You couldn't have done anything." JP thanked him and left, frustrated that he didn't learn more. He didn't know what he'd expected to find out, but all he'd established was that Sabre ran from the canyon to the shopping center, which they had already figured out. No one appeared to be chasing her, but she was obviously scared enough to keep running.

Chapter 27

Chapter 27

Wednesday evening

Sabre sat at the dining table, perusing the Madison file she'd recreated. The original was still missing. JP had gone through it earlier and jotted down notes he'd left in the first file.

JP walked in. "How are the kids?"

"Conner's in his room, working on his homework," Sabre said. "Morgan and Dené are being civil to one another, but Dené is still upset about her father coming to the party."

"Don't Dené and Travis have a visit this weekend?"

"Yes, and I hope she's willing to go. I haven't said anything more about it, nor has she. Travis wants to take her to the zoo, which she apparently likes to do. He's trying so hard to have a relationship with her, but she's pretty angry at him."

"Why?" JP asked, as he opened the refrigerator. "I know he hasn't been around for her entire life, but he didn't even know she existed. What's he supposed to do?"

"I think her real anger is at her mom for passing away, but she's not around to lash out at. So Travis gets the brunt of it."

"That's too bad." JP popped open a Pepsi. "From what I know about Travis, he wouldn't have been much of a father when she was born, but he seems pretty settled now. He's certainly the best of your aunt's kids."

"That's a pretty low bar," Sabre said. "Dené is in counseling. In fact, she has an appointment tomorrow after school. I expect, at some point, the therapist will include her father in some sessions."

"Does Travis want her to live with him?"

Sabre looked at JP's worried face. "Are you concerned that our family has grown too large too quick?"

"No, it's not that at all. If she has to stay here permanently, we'll raise her like the others. But if she were my child, I wouldn't want someone else raising her. I just can't understand a father not wanting his own kid."

"Travis has lived a bachelor's life for a lot of years, and frankly, he liked his lifestyle, but I think he does want her. He has to make sure he can give her what she needs and that she'd be happy living with him. I think it's good that they can take it slow and develop a relationship before being forced on one another."

"I'm sure you're right." JP looked at the Madison file. "Have you read through this entire thing lately?"

"I remember most of it. This is the third time Angela has been in the system. She was only two the first time. Her mother had passed out on the kitchen floor in their apartment, and Angela must've gone to get help. She was found wandering the streets. A neighbor woman about a block away saw her. Angela was able to tell the neighbor where she lived, so she took her home, discovered the mother, and called the police."

"Has there been any contact with the father since Angela was a baby?"

"No, and we don't know for certain that the man her mother named is the father. A paternity test was ordered, but he never took it. He stuck around for a few months and then disappeared. Each time the case comes back into the system, CPS does a search for him, but he's never turned up."

"What about the boyfriend the mother had living with them at the time of this last detention?" JP looked in the file. "Usher Fleming. Do you know anything about him?"

"Not much. What is it exactly you're looking for?"

"I don't know. It seems too big a coincidence that you were going to see Angela, something horrible happened to you, and now Angela's missing. There has to be a connection. I may be running 'em around the barn, but I have to do something."

"What's your plan?"

"To go through this file with a fine-tooth comb and write down every name that's mentioned. Then I'll check to see if there's any connection to Harold or to you. And I'll try to find the father and see what he's been up to. I'd also like to talk to Angela's mother. Any way you can set that up?"

"Mike Powers is her attorney. I expect he'll let you as long as you confine the questions to just this incident, and he may want to go with you. But I'm not sure you'll get very far."

"Why is that?"

"Because I talked to the social worker today and she says the mother left her program and is back on the streets."

JP's eyes widened. "Maybe she has Angela."

"That's possible. DuBois is already on it."

Chapter 28

Whursday morning

The Eddie Blane Case

Sabre met Bob at juvenile court. "Eddie is being released from the hospital and going to live with his Aunt Klara today," Sabre said. "His mother will be able to visit him in the home, and the aunt has agreed to supervise the visits. If the boy doesn't do well there, he'll be moved to a medically fragile home."

"His mother wants him with her sister even though she and her sister don't get along," Bob said. "She thinks it's best for Eddie."

They walked down the hall toward Department Four. "I really don't think this is Munchausen's," Bob said.

"Factitious Disorder, remember?"

"Yeah, whatever. I think the kid is really sick, and his doctors have failed him. His mother is pretty high strung, but she seems genuine. I'd be pretty upset with the system if my kid was sick and no one could figure it out."

"What makes you think she's telling the truth?"

"They went to the desert in Arizona a few months ago and stayed in a tent, completely isolated from anyone. Willow says that's the only time Eddie seemed to feel good. They were only supposed to stay for three days, but he was doing so well, they stayed a week. Shortly after they got home, he got sick again."

Sabre was skeptical. "Do you suppose that was because the mother didn't have anyone to get attention from?"

"Or maybe there's something in the air."

"You think it's the city air making him sick?" Sabre asked.

"I don't know." Bob stopped near the courtroom. "Sit for a second."

Sabre sat down on the bench.

Bob said, "Don't you find that strange?"

"Not if the mother is making him sick. It's perfectly logical. Has she taken him back to the desert?"

"She can't afford to take off work. They went for a weekend in Julian, but it didn't seem to work as well there, or maybe it just wasn't long enough. She'd like to move to Arizona, but she can't live in a tent in the desert. She'd still have to work, and that means the city."

A recollection hit her. "Oh my god," Sabre exclaimed. "You might be on to something."

"What?"

"My friend Jennifer has a good friend whose daughter has been sick for years with similar symptoms. They had trouble diagnosing it and blamed it on everything from attitude to MS."

"What does she have?"

"I don't remember the name, but I'll ask her, and we can do some research. I'm not saying that's what this is, but it's worth looking into."

"Thanks," Bob said. "I've been trying to skim through the medical records, but there's a ton."

"I know. Me too. I would have JP do it, but he's too wrapped up in what happened to me. You know what we need on this case?" Before Bob could answer, she said, "A Court Appointed Special Advocate. Someone who can give it a lot of time."

"Maybe, but sometimes the CASA volunteers just rubber stamp the social worker's recommendations, and we don't need that."

"And sometimes they do their jobs. I've had some really good ones on cases. I'm putting this on calendar for tomorrow if I can. I'll request someone with medical knowledge. Maybe we'll get a retired nurse or something."

"Fat chance," Bob said.

"Could it be something as simple as mold in the home?"

"That was my first thought because things seem to be worse since she's lived in that house, but the mother had the house checked from top to bottom for mold, even inside the walls."

"Are you sure she did it?"

"She's got paperwork to prove it, and the social worker followed up on it. It's legit."

"I thought that was too easy."

"So, what's going on with your brain?" Bob asked. "Have you remembered anything else?"

"No, just that glimpse of someone pulling me out of the car. I've been doing meditation to relax my mind, but so far, it hasn't worked."

"Have you thought about hypnosis?" Bob asked.

"Does that work?"

"I don't know, but it's basically a deep form of relaxation, right?"

"I'll do some research." Sabre stood. "There's Powers. I need to talk to him." She walked toward an attorney who was about to go into the courtroom.

"Hey, Mike, got a minute?"

"Sure, what's up?" He let go of the door and stepped toward Sabre.

"Angela Madison has disappeared."

"Yeah, the social worker notified me. Is there something I can do to help?"

"JP is investigating for me, and he'd like to talk to the mother if you're okay with that."

"Do you think Angela is with Xander?"

"It's not likely, but still possible. JP is looking for other bad actors that Angela may have come into contact with while living with her mother."

"I'm fine with him talking to her, *if* he can find her. She's back on the streets, so it may not be easy. Tell JP to call me, and I'll give him whatever information I have."

Chapter 29

Chapter 29

Thursday morning

After hearing from Sabre, JP immediately called Attorney Mike Powers.

"What can you tell me about Angela's father?" JP asked.

"Not much more than is in the report," Powers said. "The guy she claims to be the father hasn't been around since shortly after Angela was born. He could be anywhere, or he could be dead. No one has seen him in years."

"You say that like you don't think he's the father."

"Who knows? Xander has always stuck to that story, but she was using and hooking at the time Angela was conceived, so it could be any number of men."

"Do you have any idea where she might be?" JP asked.

"She has a couple of men friends she spends time with. I think one is her drug supplier, and the other is a john. I was surprised the john stuck with her, if in fact he has." Powers hesitated.

"Why? Is it someone we know?"

"No, but he's fairly well-off and could buy just about any sex worker he wanted. She says he likes women 'a little on the trashy side,' but she gets pretty bad when she's using. It may not even be true. Maybe Xander made the whole thing up, although she provided specific details when she told me, and she was clean at the time."

"That is odd."

"If I give you this information, you have to do two things."

"What are they?" JP asked.

"Only use it to find Angela or figure out what happened to Sabre."

"That's a promise. What's the second thing?"

"If you find the mother and she has Angela, let me know so I can maneuver my client through the court system a little gentler."

"I can do that. But if Angela is in danger, I will rescue her first."

"That's understood."

After Powers gave him the names, JP did a quick search on the internet. The drug supplier, Curtis Ivers, had Instagram and Facebook accounts. Both contained photos of him, many of which portrayed him as a dealer. There were no actual images of drug deals going down, but lots of innuendo. He'd also posted photos of people shooting up. JP wondered if they were his clientele. *This guy was not too bright.*

Alex Griffin, the john friend, was a different story. His only social media account was LinkedIn. He owned a house in La Jolla and worked as a program manager for Boeing. *What was he doing with Xander?* JP continued to search for useful information about the men for a while, but soon got restless.

In his truck, he headed to an area near downtown where Curtis Ivers seemed to hang out. JP figured it was his most likely chance of finding Xander.

At midday, the neighborhood was pretty quiet. He walked around for a while and decided to return later that night when there would be more action. If Xander was there she was probably asleep, especially if she was working the streets again.

He drove over to Boeing to see Griffin, hoping he could catch him at work. He walked into the building and approached the receptionist, a thirty-something, attractive brunette.

"I'd like to see Alex Griffin, please."

"Do you have an appointment?"

"I don't."

"What company are you with?"

"I'm a private investigator. My name is JP Torn." He handed her a card.

The receptionist picked up the phone and said, "There's a PI here to see Mr. Griffin."

The receptionist stood and said, "Follow me." She led JP through large double doors, then pointed to a small office. "That's Mr. Griffin's assistant, Mrs. Lewis. She'll be able to help you."

The receptionist left, and JP walked through the open office door and approached the desk. A tall, thin woman with salt-and-pepper hair in a Veronica Lake style looked up. "You want to see Mr. Griffin?"

"Correct."

"What's this about?"

"It's personal."

"You'll need to give me more than that. He's a busy man."

"I work for Attorney Sabre Brown, and I need to see Mr. Griffin about a case."

"Does it actually involve him?"

"He knows some of the people." The woman still didn't make any attempt to contact her boss. "Tell him it's about Xander and Angela," JP pressed.

The gatekeeper finally placed a call. She explained who he was, said, "Okay" and hung up. She stood and opened the door. "Mr. Griffin is busy this morning, but he'll see you as soon as he can." She pointed to chairs outside her office. "Please wait there. His office is just down the hall. One of us will get you when he's ready."

JP sat down and checked the time, then looked around at the wall décor, all aviation related. Five minutes passed. JP walked down the hall, looking at photos and reading the captions. They started with a copy of a drawing made in 1480 by Leonardo da Vinci of his ornithopter flying machine, an aircraft that would theoretically fly by flapping its wings. The pictures formed a timeline as they modernized. When JP was almost to the end, where a Boeing jet loomed on the wall, a tall man in a suit stepped out of an office. JP moved toward him.

"Mr. Torn? Please come in."

"Thank you." JP stepped inside, and Griffin asked him to sit.

JP again explained that he was an investigator.

"You said this was about Xander and Angela?"

"Yes, that's correct."

Griffin seemed relatively calm except he rubbed his five o'clock shadow in a nervous gesture. Then he said, "I'm getting a jump on *no-shave November*," adding, "The goal is to grow awareness of cancer prevention. Because many cancer patients lose their hair. Then you donate the money typically spent on shaving to prevent cancer."

"I've heard about it. That's a great idea." JP moved on. "How well do you know Xander and Angela?"

"I've known them quite a while. Has something happened?"

"When did you last see Xander?"

"About a week ago."

"Do you know what's going on in her life right now?" JP wanted to find out how much the guy knew before he explained anything about the case.

"I know she's using again, and that Angela is living with her aunt. Is Angela okay?"

"She's disappeared."

Griffin stood, raising his voice. "What do you mean *disappeared*?"

JP was surprised by his reaction and deeply curious about this man's involvement in their lives. *He seemed so respectable. How did he get mixed up with Xander?*

"Angela's aunt took her to school, but she never went to class, and she wasn't there when Jan went to pick her up."

"That's horrible," Griffin said. "What can I do to help?"

"Do you know where Xander is now?"

"Like I said, I haven't seen her in a week, but at that time she was staying with someone named Terry in an apartment in the East Village area." Griffin sounded distressed. "I can get you the address, but I don't know if she's still there. When she's using, she moves around a lot, probably because no one can put up with her for long."

"Have you ever known Angela to run off?"

"She's adventurous and likes to wander, but she would've come home if she were able. Do you think she's with Xander?"

"It's possible, which is why we need to find her. Angela can't be safe with her mother if she's on the streets."

Griffin rubbed his chin again, but didn't speak.

"How long have you known Xander?" JP was having a hard time believing this man was her customer. It was possible Powers got it wrong, but you could never know what people did in their personal lives.

"We met when we were both kids, then got reacquainted a few years ago." He paused. "You're wondering why, aren't you? Why I would be friends with Xander?"

"It don't take a genius to spot a goat in a flock of sheep."

Griffin smiled. "You're right. But she wasn't always like this. When she's clean, Xander's a likable person. I've tried to help her and Angela the last couple of years. Xander has had some rough times, and Angela suffers because of it."

"Does that mean you won't tell me?"

"How we know each other isn't important, but I'll always be there for them. If Xander decides to tell you, I'm fine with that. But our relationship is in no way relevant to Angela's disappearance."

JP switched gears. "Do you know anything about Angela's father?"

"Why? Do you think he might have her?"

"In cases like this, more often than not, it's a parent."

Griffin either didn't know anything about Angela's father or chose not to tell. JP asked a few more questions, then thanked him, and left. His next move was to find 'someone named Terry' in a sleazy part of town.

Chapter 30

Thursday late morning

JP drove to East Village, which sat between downtown San Diego and Sherman Heights. The neighborhood had a high crime rate and heavy drug usage. Homeless people and heroin addicts filled the area. Even though it had a high police presence, they were far outnumbered by the criminals. JP had visited the neighborhood many times in search of other clients who were using or selling drugs.

Still wondering how a man like Griffin got tied up with Xander, JP went to the address Griffin had given him, a dilapidated apartment building that looked like it hadn't been painted in fifty years. The concrete steps were bordering on dangerous. The edge of the first one was completely broken off, and huge cracks ran through the rest. A homeless man lay in the bushes next to the stairs, his shopping cart tied to his leg.

JP found the correct apartment and knocked.

A minute later, a sleepy-eyed man opened the door. "What do you want?" he asked nonchalantly, trying to adjust his eyes to the sunlight.

"Are you Terry?"

"Yeah, that's me."

"I'm looking for Xander Madison. Is she here?"

"Nope."

"When did you last see her?"

"I don't know." His words were slurred. "A couple of days ago, I guess."

"Are you sure she's not here?" JP insisted. "I was told she was here, and it's important that I find her. It's about her daughter."

"She ain't here, man."

"Her daughter is missing," JP said. "If the girl is here and you hide her, you could be in a lot of trouble."

"I have a daughter too. I'd be pretty upset if she was missing."

JP wanted to punch him. He could only imagine what a loser this father was to his kid.

Terry moved aside. "Come in and look for yourself."

JP stepped into the dark room. Without thinking, he reached for the light switch and turned it on. The man flinched.

"Sorry, but I couldn't see."

The room was a mess, dirty clothes all around, empty fast-food packages, ashtrays full of butts. And it smelled as bad as it looked. Smoke, spoiled food, and urine permeated the air. A man lay passed out on the sofa.

"She ain't here," Terry said, moving toward the hall. "Look." He opened an interior door. The bedroom looked and smelled worse than the living room. JP followed him inside and checked the closets. No one was there. Then he checked the bathroom. Still nothing.

JP took a business card from his pocket, wrote Powers' number on the back, and handed it to Terry. "It's important that we find Xander's daughter. If you see Xander, please have her call me, or if she doesn't want to talk to me, have her call her attorney. I wrote his number on the back of my card."

"Sure, man."

JP left and walked around the neighborhood. It was likely Xander hadn't gone too far, and if Angela was ever in Terry's apartment, someone might have seen her. He spent the next half hour talking to neighbors and showing Angela's photo, but no one reported seeing either of them.

JP called DuBois and told him about Terry.

"What are you doing, McCloud?" DuBois sounded annoyed. "If Terry knows something, you've tipped him off, and he probably won't talk now."

"I can't help it if I'm two steps ahead of you. Besides, that guy is so out of it, he likely won't remember I was there or care if he does. He invited me into his apartment and let me look around. He had no idea who I was."

"How did you find out about Terry?" DuBois asked.

"That I can't tell you."

"At least we know the area where Xander hangs out. I'll make sure the officers who patrol that neighborhood keep an eye out for Angela." In the background, DuBois shuffled papers. "I have to go. I have a couple of things that are pressing, but I'm hungry. Do you want to meet at In-N-Out in an hour for a quick bite? We can compare notes."

"See you then." JP hung up and checked his watch. He still had forty minutes to kill until he had to leave. He decided to keep looking for Xander and Angela. He walked the streets, checking in every alley and questioning people, most of whom were homeless. But no one had seen, or admitted to having seen, either of them. JP finally gave up, hoping to have better luck that evening.

Chapter 31

Thursday afternoon

"Gunner's not our man," DuBois said. He sat across from JP at a table outside where they could talk, a burger in hand.

"How do you know?" JP noticed dark circles under the detective's eyes.

"I went to the bars Gunner frequents and started asking questions. The bartender and waitress who served him at the Hay Bale both said he arrived somewhere around four-thirty, or five at the latest, and stayed until nine."

"And they're certain he never left?"

"They're certain. Especially the waitress, who can't stand Gunner. She said he hits on her all the time, even gets hands-on sometimes. He shot pool, drank, and hit on the women, the same thing he does every time he comes in. They did mention that he came in earlier than usual and took longer to get a woman to leave with him."

"That man is as worthless as a side saddle on a sow," JP said. "What else you got?"

"Porter claims he was with a friend, but we haven't been able to track down his alibi. You got anything more on Lynch?"

"I spoke to his neighbor, the cop. He said Lynch came home on Tuesday, and they had a casual conversation. Lynch claims he was camping in Big Bear, but who knows if that's the truth.

Even if he did camp there, he still could've driven to San Diego and back Friday night. It's only a couple of hours away."

"So, he's not off the list."

"My real concern right now is Angela," JP said. "Did anyone at school see her yesterday?"

"The teacher on duty in front of the school says she saw the aunt drop her off, but then Angela blended into a crowd of students." DuBois paused to take another bite of his meal. "The teacher vented about the inconsiderate parents who drop their kids off and then speed off like there are no other kids around. Then she went back to directing traffic for the other parents. No other staff saw Angela, so it's likely she didn't make it inside."

"What about her friends?"

"No one saw her, or they're not talking. Even her self-proclaimed best friend, Nevaeh Powell, claims she didn't see Angela and doesn't know where she is."

JP raised an eyebrow. "You say that like you don't believe her."

"She seemed nervous, so maybe she's hiding something, but she's a kid. It's possible she's just scared or worried about her friend. According to Nevaeh, they're really close, so if she saw something suspicious, I'm sure she would've said something. But the friend could also be keeping a secret she swore not to tell."

"You mean if Angela is on an adventure?"

"That's a possibility, or maybe she knows something but doesn't think it's important. I'm kind of grasping at straws here." DuBois had finished his burger and now had his head in his hands. "I get edgy when I have to deal with missing or endangered kids. I don't know how you and Sabre do it every day."

"I'd like to say you get used to it, but you don't. Yet every once in a while, you feel like you really help some kid, and that makes up for it." JP paused to take a bite. "Maybe Sabre could talk to the friend. She has a way of getting information out of kids that no one else can."

"It couldn't hurt. It might be easiest to talk to her at school, but I'll text you her home address just in case."

JP gathered up his trash. "What's next?"

"I'm not officially on Angela's case, but the Juvenile Services Team is keeping me informed, and I'll follow up anything that looks connected to Sabre. I've hit a dead end on Harold's murder. Sabre hasn't remembered anything else, has she?"

"No, but you'll be the first to know when she does." JP stood. "Time to head to the barn."

They cleaned up their table, then walked toward their cars.

"Did they find Angela's father?" JP asked.

"Not yet. They've thrown out a wide net for him, but don't get your hopes up."

JP stopped at his truck. "You're looking pretty tired, my friend."

"Humph." DuBois forced a smile. "I haven't slept much since I got this case. Getting too old for this, I guess. I used to be able to run on pure adrenaline, but not so much now."

"Is there anything else I can do to help?"

"You're doing plenty already. Don't worry. I'll be fine."

Chapter 32

Chapter 32

Thursday afternoon

Sabre waited alone in the principal's office for Nevaeh. She hadn't been there long when Ms. Sauer returned with the child.

"Ms. Brown, this is Nevaeh."

"Hi, I'm Angela's attorney and friend."

"I'll leave you two alone," Ms. Sauer said.

"Are you sure you don't want us to go somewhere else so you can use your office?" Sabre asked.

"It's fine. You'll have more privacy here, and I have a few classrooms to visit. Just let the secretary know when you're done."

Ms. Sauer left, and Sabre took a seat close to Nevaeh. "Your hair is so pretty."

"My mom did the cornrows for me. I like to hear the jingle from the beads when I shake my head." She moved her head from side to side.

"That does sound fun."

"My mom says if I'm feeling sad, I should just shake my head and listen to the beads sing to me."

"Are you feeling sad about something now?" Sabre asked.

"I miss Angela."

"I miss her too. We're doing everything we can to find her. That's why I wanted to talk to you."

"I told that detective that I don't know where she is."

"Sometimes we know things and don't realize it."

"How?" Nevaeh looked confused.

"Angela may have told you a secret that would help us find her, but you don't want to tell because you made a promise to her."

Nevaeh looked down at her feet but didn't speak.

"Angela may be in trouble if we don't find her soon. We don't know if someone took her, or if she went off on her own. But even if she went on an adventure, she shouldn't be out there by herself. Maybe she can't get home now, or she's lost."

Nevaeh squirmed but still said nothing.

"Tell me what you like about Angela."

Nevaeh looked up and smiled. "She's so much fun. She enjoys playing dress up, and I like that too. We both want to be actresses when we grow up, but Angela's great at it. She says you have to believe you are the character you're playing. That's pretty smart, huh?"

"Very smart. She seems like a natural, but that doesn't mean you can't be just as good. Some of us have to work harder at things to get there, but in the end, you can still reach your goal if you want it bad enough."

"You think so?"

"I do. You just have to practice a lot."

"I really want to be an actress someday. Before Angela came to this school, I didn't have anyone who really understood me like she does. But she's braver than I am."

"How so?"

"She's not afraid of much."

"Is that why she's gone now? Because she's doing something she wasn't afraid to do?"

The girl looked down again.

"Nevaeh, it's important that we know where Angela is so we can help her."

She shook her head, and the beads tinkled. "I don't know where she is. Really."

"But you do know something, don't you?"

Her head stayed down. "She said she had to help her mom, but she didn't tell me where she was going."

"Did she say anything else about her mother?"

"Just that she was sick. But Angela had an idea that could help her. She said she knew somewhere she could go to get help."

"Did Angela say where that was?"

"No."

"Did she mention any other people?"

"No, but it sounded like she knew someone who would help her."

"What makes you think that?"

The girl shrugged. "I don't know, just the way she talked."

Sabre wondered if Angela meant a place or a person. Maybe she wanted to get her mom into a shelter. *Had Angela talked to her lately?* Sabre decided to ask the aunt when the last contact was. "When did Angela tell you this?" Sabre asked.

"Tuesday at school."

"Did you see her yesterday?"

She shook her head. "I usually get to school after her, and she waits for me by the flagpole, but when I got there, she wasn't there. I waited until the bell rang, then I left. I thought she was sick or something, until the cop started asking me questions."

"You've been a big help. Thank you." Sabre handed her a business card. "I spoke with your mother earlier, and she knows I talked to you. She wants us to find Angela, so I'm sure she'll let you call me if you think of anything else. Please call even if you don't think it's important, but especially if you think of any names Angela mentioned."

"I hope you find her, Ms. Brown."

"We'll do our best."

Chapter 33

Thursday night

JP parked a block from Terry's apartment and walked toward Market Street, checking every nook and cranny in the Gaslamp district. He questioned every homeless person and stopped in every bar, but found no sign of Xander or Angela. Up and down Sixth Avenue, he continued the search. He took E Street over to Fifth and was headed south when he spotted DuBois.

"What are you doing here?" JP asked.

"Same thing you are, looking for Xander and Angela. Any luck?"

"They seem to be as lost as last year's Easter eggs."

"That's one way of putting it, McCloud." DuBois gave a half smile. "I'm pretty certain they're not around here. I've spoken to three officers who are searching as well. They did the same last night, and no one has seen Xander since Angela went missing."

"You think they're together?" JP asked as they walked. He noticed DuBois moved slower than usual.

"I guess maybe I want to assume that. It's better than thinking the girl was abducted, even though I'm certain being with her mother is not safe either. At least not for very long. It would give us a better chance of finding her than if she's with some stranger. But still, it's not unusual for druggies to disappear for a few days, even a week at a time."

"Should we call it a night?" JP asked. "You look exhausted."

"You're right, it's time to leave. There's plenty of officers looking for them, and they'll let me know the minute they have information." DuBois blinked. "Where's your truck?"

"On Market near Seventeenth."

"Geez, McCloud, you covered a lot of ground. Come on, I'm right around the corner. I'll give you a ride back."

They got in DuBois' car and drove west. "You're going home, right?" JP asked.

"I am, but I think I'll stop at the Hay Bale and see if Porter Holloway happens to be there. It's on the way. I only live a few miles from there."

JP was tired too and wanted to go home, but said, "How about if I join you? I'll take my truck and meet you there."

"Sounds good. We can have a beer and unwind."

They reached the spot where JP had parked. "I'm not sure I'd leave my truck in this area," DuBois said. "You might not have tires. I'll wait to make sure you can drive away."

"Thanks." JP walked around the truck, found nothing amiss, then got in and started the engine. He rolled down his window. "I think we're good. See you at the roadhouse."

Chapter 34

Chapter 34

Thursday night

JP met DuBois near the door, and they walked into the tavern. They worked their way toward an empty table with a view of the pool tables and a small dance floor.

"It's pretty crowded in here for a Thursday night, don't you think?" JP asked.

"Apparently the place keeps hopping," DuBois said. "They have special events every weeknight and live music on weekends. Tuesday and Wednesday, they have pool tournaments."

"What's happening tonight?"

"Karaoke. But they're on a break right now. Want to put your name in?"

JP laughed. "I'll pass. Do you come here often?"

"No. I'm not really a country music fan. The first time I came here was to ask about Gunner. I heard Porter shows up a lot too, especially on Thursdays."

JP shook his head. "How can you *not* be a country fan?"

"That was your takeaway from what I just said?"

"Yeah. Country is the best music ever."

"Of course, you'd like it, McCloud." DuBois glanced around. "This whole place is filled with McClouds. You must feel right at home."

"I'll go get a couple of beers," JP said. "It may be a while before the waitress gets around to us. You sit and relax."

DuBois didn't argue, and JP walked away. He passed the pool tables and saw Porter playing against a short guy with glasses. JP watched him take a shot, then moved on.

JP returned with the beers and set them on the table. "Porter's playing pool. He's all decked out in boots, hat, and shiny belt buckle. I wonder if he's ever ridden a horse."

DuBois leaned over and looked toward the pool tables. "Looks like he just won that game. You any good at pool, McCloud?"

"I've been known to win a game or two."

"Think you can beat Porter?"

"From the shot I saw him take, my dog could beat him."

"Let's go."

They started to get up and noticed Porter walking toward the stage near the dance floor.

"Wait," JP said. "I think he's going to sing."

They sat down and listened to Porter belt out a rendition of Brett Young's *Mercy*.

"Is that how the song is supposed to sound?" DuBois asked.

"No, that was horrible. It's one of my favorite songs, and he just ruined it for me. How can those girls be clapping and screaming for that?"

"They want the singer, not the voice."

JP shook his head.

They waited until Porter went back to the pool tables, then walked over.

"Anyone up for a game?" JP asked, looking straight at Porter.

"I don't mind beating you, old man," Porter said. He eyed JP with recognition, then grabbed his pool stick.

JP just smiled. It had been a while since he played. One thing he had learned long ago was to not talk smack until the game was over, and only then, if it was called for.

"I hope you shoot better than you sing," a drunk man called out.

Porter turned, stepped right into the man's face, and uttered a string of profanity.

"Come on," JP said. "You gonna play or fight?"

Porter shoved the man, and he stumbled off.

DuBois took a step closer to Porter.

"Back off, copper," Porter said. "I ain't done nothing wrong. Unless you wanna arrest *me* for that guy being too drunk to stand upright."

"Just keep your hands to yourself." DuBois stepped aside so JP and Porter could get to the table.

"Go ahead," JP said to Porter. "You can break."

"I don't need any favors. We'll lag for it."

"What's that?" JP asked, as if he didn't know.

Porter rolled his eyes. "We both shoot the little white ball to the end of the table, and when it comes back, whoever gets the closest to this end goes first." His tone was thick with sarcasm. "We'll use a second ball and do it at the same time." He shook his head and set up the lag balls. "This ain't gonna be much of a game."

The waitress approached, and Porter stopped to leer at her. "You're lookin' sweet tonight, honey." She ignored him and asked JP for his order. He declined. When she started to walk away, Porter said, "I'll take another beer, sweet cheeks." She nodded, took a few more drink orders, and walked off.

Porter watched her go, looking her up and down. "That's yummy." He turned to JP. "You ready to lag?"

"I'm ready."

They took shots at the same time and both hit the head rail. Porter's ball came back faster, hit the foot rail and rolled about four inches. JP's returned to the foot rail and stopped less than an inch from the end.

"Lucky jerk," Porter snarled.

"*Now,* you can break," JP said.

"You won the lag, you idiot."

"I know. That gives me the choice, right?"

Porter's face turned red, and his neck muscles bulged. DuBois couldn't help but smile at his indignation.

Porter put two balls in with the break, one odd and one even. He called for odd and put one more ball in a pocket before he missed his shot. When JP took his turn, he ran the table, making shots that surprised him. A crowd gathered to watch and encourage JP, making Porter livid. JP sunk the eight ball and smiled.

"You hustled me," Porter whined.

The waitress returned with the drinks, and Porter started flirting inappropriately with her. She kept walking away from him, but he followed as she passed out each drink. When he grabbed one of her butt cheeks, JP moved toward them, with DuBois right behind.

"Leave me alone," the waitress said.

"What's the matter, Angel? You only service old men, like my daddy?"

"Knock it off," JP said.

Porter spun around and swung a fist. JP ducked, and the punch caught DuBois on the side of his head. JP grabbed Porter's arm, twisted it behind his back, and shoved him face down on a pool table.

"Don't let your mouth write checks that your ass can't cash," JP said, as DuBois slapped cuffs on the punk.

"What the hell?" Porter mumbled.

They walked him outside, and DuBois took off the handcuffs. "How much have you had to drink?"

"Only what you saw at the tables. I don't drink before I sing. I do a better job sober."

I can't imagine what you sound like after a few beers, JP thought.

"Go home, cool off, and quit making a fool of yourself," DuBois said.

"Who do you think you are?" Porter asked.

"Really? That's your response?" DuBois dangled the handcuffs he was still holding.

Porter raised his hands, palms out. "Okay." No apology. No remorse.

"Go on. Get out of here before I change my mind."

Porter strutted toward the parking lot.

"What was that all about?" JP asked.

"I want him to know I'm watching him."

"But he punched you. You could've arrested him."

"Yeah, but then I'd have a whole lot of paperwork to do."

Chapter 35

Chapter 35

Friday morning

"I understand you set this special hearing, Ms. Brown. Is that correct?" Judge Hekman peered over her glasses.

"Yes, Your Honor. I think Eddie would benefit from a Court Appointed Special Advocate. Since there are so many medical records to sift through, it would be helpful if the worker has some medical background, if that's possible."

"Are there any objections to a CASA being appointed?" the judge asked.

"None, Your Honor, on behalf of the mother," Bob said.

"No, Your Honor," County Counsel Dave Casey said, "on behalf of the Department."

"The court orders a Court Appointed Special Advocate be appointed on this case if one is available. Preferably one with some medical background."

"Thank you, Your Honor," Sabre said. "And there's one more thing."

"Yes?"

"If this child is actually sick, and we miss it, we will have failed him. So, I did some research and discovered several diseases that fit Eddie's symptoms but are rare and hard to detect. One such disease is myalgic encephalomyelitis, otherwise known as chronic fatigue syndrome. It's a long-term illness that often goes undiagnosed and affects many body systems. Patients often have sleep problems, pain, and dizziness." Sabre paused to let the judge absorb the information. "An estimated 836,000 to 2.5 million Americans suffer from ME/CFS, but most have not been officially diagnosed. This is only one such disease that fits Eddie's symptoms. There are many others that have no definitive test, yet affect hundreds of thousands, if not millions, of people. While the court has jurisdiction, we need to make sure we don't decide anything until we've exhausted all avenues."

"Are you asking that Eddie be tested for this disease? And is the test invasive?"

"There is no scientific test available at this time, Your Honor, so no. However, I'd like the court order to reflect that I receive notice prior to any tests or treatments for Eddie and full access to his doctors."

"So ordered."

Bob started to leave the courtroom. Sabre touched his arm and said, "We have another case in here."

"I know, but I'm not ready on that. I have an *in-custody* case, and I have to talk to my client first."

"Okay. I have a couple of cases to do in Department Three, and then I'll see you back here when you're ready."

~~~

Sabre finished her calendar except for the case in Department Four. On her way back to that courtroom, she was paged to the Voices for Children office.

"We have a CASA volunteer for you on the Blane case," the director said.

"Wow, that was quick."

"He's a perfect fit and has been eager for this kind of case." She handed Sabre a paper with the man's name and phone number. "He has already been notified and accepted the appointment. He's coming in to pick up the file this afternoon. It's his first case, but he has plenty of time and enthusiasm."
~~~

Sabre thanked her and walked out, reading the name as she left. "Hmm," she murmured.

At Department Four, she peeked in to see if Bob was there yet. He wasn't, so she sat on the bench and waited.

He showed up ten minutes later. "I'm ready, Sobs."

"They're still doing a hearing, and I don't know what's taking so long."

Bob sat down on the bench next to her.

"Guess what? A CASA was appointed on the Blane case," Sabre said.

"Already? That was fast."

"That's exactly what I said. But this guy has been waiting for the right case, and this was it. Wait until you see who it is."

"Is it someone we know?"

"Not personally, but he's a retired doctor."

"So, you got your wish." Bob grinned. "While you're on a roll, could you wish that I win the lottery?"

"Sure," Sabre said. "I would've been happy with a licensed vocational nurse, but we kind of hit the mother lode. He's a retired pediatrician who couldn't stand being idle any longer."

"I don't know if I like that. Doctors don't like to go against other doctors, and a dozen doctors on this case have said Eddie's fine. Do you really think this guy will go against them?"

"He doesn't work with them, so he can be objective, and that's what I'm looking for. Besides, aren't you stereotyping a little? For gosh sakes, Bob, your father's a doctor. How can you say that?"

"That's why I can say it."

"Well, he's what we have, and we need to work with him. We'll just have to keep his feet to the fire." Sabre fiddled with the paper she was holding.

"What are you thinking, Sobs?"

"I might go to a hypnotist to see if I can get my memory back," she blurted, concerned Bob might not approve. Not that it would stop her, but she valued his opinion.

Bob gave her a skeptical look.

"I take it you don't think it's a good idea."

"My dad's a doctor, remember? I grew up with science as the answer to everything. I'm not sure what I think about it. My dad would say hypnosis is hocus pocus, but I don't know."

"What could it hurt?"

"It could hurt if you think you remember and you really don't."

"If it gives JP and DuBois something to investigate, it could lead to something. Regardless of how I get my memory back now, it could be suspect. In a courtroom, a defense attorney would have a field day impeaching me."

"Which is why you have a better chance if you come up with memories on your own."

"It's not like I'm seeing a fortune teller. The hypnotist isn't going to plant ideas in my brain. She's only going to make me relax enough to hopefully let the memories out. And if they help the investigation, it's worth it."

"It sounds like you already have it set up."

"I'm seeing someone this afternoon at two o'clock."

"Well, if it works, whatever you remember could provide a lead that makes the difference. Just don't expect too much. There's a good chance it won't work at all."

Chapter 36

Friday morning

JP pulled his truck into the campground at Big Bear. He was a long way from home, but he didn't know what to do next, and he was never one to *take a tater and wait.* At least he could follow up on Todd Lynch, either confirm or eliminate him as a suspect. It had been years since Sabre was on his case, but Lynch continued to carry a misplaced grudge. He was a coward. That was evident in the way he treated his children and the way he harassed Sabre with his emails and social media posts. You never knew when a man like that would go off.

There was a space near the campground office, so JP parked and walked inside. A brunette with gray roots and autumn-brown eyes stood behind the counter. A man about the same age stood nearby.

"Good morning," the woman said. "What can we do for you?"

"I'm JP Torn. This is a mighty nice park you have."

"Thank you. Are you looking for a space? It's not too crowded this time of year. Summer is over, and the snow hasn't hit us yet, so we're kind of between seasons."

"I'm here on business, investigating a missing child case." He didn't feel the need to get into the whole thing, and missing children usually got plenty of sympathy.

"I'm Pat Simmons, and this is my husband, Oliver. We've owned the park for fifteen years. What can we help you with?"

"Do you know a man named Todd Lynch?"

Concern flashed on her face. "Is one of those sweet little boys missing?"

"No," JP said, "but I take it you know their father."

"Yes, he's been coming here for years."

"When did you last see him?"

"He just left a few days ago. Let me check." She turned to her computer and within a minute said, "He checked in on Thursday and left Tuesday."

"Did you check him in?"

"Yes. I remember because I asked him about the boys. He said he was alone this time, just needed a little getaway by himself. I was disappointed, because I like seeing the boys, especially the two younger ones. The older one is more like his father."

"What do you mean?"

"He's not as pleasant, shall we say, as the other two."

Oliver stepped up to the counter. "Pat, he doesn't want to hear all that." He lowered his voice to a whisper, but JP still heard what he said. "Todd may be his client for all you know."

"I don't care who he works for," Pat argued. "Todd Lynch is an obnoxious jerk, and he's mean to those boys."

"I don't work for Mr. Lynch," JP said. "And I've seen him around his kids."

"He's a terrible father," Pat said. "And those boys are scared to death of him."

"What does Todd have to do with the missing child?" Oliver asked.

"I don't know at this point, but he might've been in the area where the child vanished. I'm not accusing him, but at this point, I'm following up on every lead or witness."

"When did this happen?"

"I'm trying to establish where Lynch was on Friday night. Did either of you see him that night?"

"I saw him when he checked in on Thursday. Later that night, he was drinking and playing horseshoes with other guys in the camp. They got loud, and Oliver had to tell them to keep the noise down."

"Did you see him after that?"

"He came into the office Friday morning and got coffee. That was his usual routine. I think he did that each morning he was here."

"Did you see him later in the day or Friday evening?"

"No, but that doesn't mean he wasn't here."

Oliver's expression changed as if he were deep in thought. JP pivoted to him. "How about you, Oliver? Did you see him?"

"No. I didn't. I always walk the campground a few times in the evening before I go to bed. A few families were sitting outside and talking, but I didn't see Todd. But he could've still been there, you know."

"What time was your last walk?"

"Around nine o'clock." Oliver's brow wrinkled, as if he remembered something.

"What are you thinking?" JP asked.

"His car wasn't where he usually parks Friday night. He's always concerned that someone might dent or scratch his car, so he parks it in the same spot. It was parked there on Thursday, and I know it was there on Sunday. I wasn't around much on Saturday, so I don't know about that day. But that doesn't mean he wasn't here. He could've parked the car somewhere else, and I didn't notice."

"Has he ever done that before?"

They both shook their heads. "Not in the fifteen years he's been coming here," Oliver said.

JP thanked them and drove into town to check out the local bars. He was still no closer to determining if Lynch was involved. JP stopped at the first tavern he came to, but no one knew Lynch or remembered seeing him. He tried several others and got the same response. A few didn't have the same employees working who had worked Friday night. Other bartenders said it was just too busy to remember anyone who wasn't a regular. JP discovered there were at least ten bars within a two-mile radius, with many more on the outskirts or in neighboring towns. After the sixth stop, he gave up and started home.

JP had hoped he'd find something more concrete on Lynch. He couldn't stand the guy, but if Lynch had a real alibi, they could've crossed him off their list. At this point, he was still a suspect.

Chapter 37

Chapter 37

Friday afternoon

Sabre opened the door to the hypnotherapist's office and entered a narrow, L-shaped room. The smell of lavender filled the air, a water dispenser stood against the wall, and the four chairs were empty. Smooth music and soft lighting set the mood for relaxation.

Sabre was five minutes early, so she sat down. Shortly, an attractive, blonde woman about ten years older than her approached. She spoke softly, then led Sabre down the hall to an office on the end.

Once inside, she used a normal tone to introduce herself as Tara. She was friendly and soft-spoken and attempted to put Sabre at ease. This was a first for her, and Sabre didn't know if the process would actually work, but she had to do something. It could take months, or years, to get her memory back, if she ever did. By then, the trail would be cold. She needed this to be effective.

Sabre explained more thoroughly what had happened, and Tara schooled her on the process for hypnosis.

"Don't expect to have a flood of memories today. Although that could happen, it's not likely. When there has been a traumatic experience and you repress it, your conscious mind does not want to remember. And the more stress you're under, the less likely you will remember it." Tara smiled gently.

"So, the best we can do is get you to relax, which is what hypnosis is all about, a state of deep relaxation. Later, you'll likely remember things at odd times, when you least expect to. Times when you're in a relaxed state, doing something you enjoy, and your mind is free to let it out. Any questions?"

"How many visits will this require?"

"It's hard to say, but I'll give you a tape of our session today, and you can listen to it at home. I'll also give you some trigger words to help you relax any time during the day. We can schedule another appointment for next week, and if you need it, you can come in. If not, you can cancel it."

"Okay. I'm ready."

Tara asked Sabre to get comfortable, either lying or sitting comfortably on the sofa. Sabre chose to lie down. Then she hypnotized her and tested her to see if she would raise and lower her arms on command, which she did.

"I want you to find a spot on the ceiling and stare at it. Now, using only your eyes and your peripheral vision, look to the left and right and up and down, as far as you can see. I'll count down from ten, and when I say a number, your eyes will open. When I snap my fingers, your eyes will close." Tara paused, and music played quietly in the background. "Ten, eyes open." She snapped her fingers. "Eyes closed. Nine, eyes open." She snapped her fingers again. The hypnotherapist continued all the way to zero. "Eyes closed."

Sabre could feel her body relax and begin to tingle. Then a weight lifted from her shoulders as she went deeper into a hypnotic state. She remained aware of everything that was said, including the commands to remember what had happened, but no repressed memory came to her.

Before Tara brought her out of the deep sleep, she gave Sabre anchor words to help her relax anytime she felt stressed. "Take a deep breath in through your nose, and when you exhale through your mouth, think or say the word *calm*." She did the same for the words *relax* and *in control*.

"In a moment, I'll count up to five, and at five, your eyes will open, and you will awaken completely. You will feel like you just woke up from a long nap. Up to one—still physically relaxed. Up to two—still emotionally calm. Up to three—more mentally alert. Four—starting to open the eyes. They may flutter a little. And five means eyes open, wide awake. One, two, three, four, five—eyes open, wide awake, good job."

Sabre eyes fluttered, then opened without her control. She lay there for a few seconds and then sat up.

"How do you feel?"

"Rested, but a little disappointed. I know you said not to expect too much, but I still hoped it would flood back to me."

Chapter 38

FRiday night

Sabre walked into the house, frustrated she hadn't gained more from her hypnotherapist session, worried about Angela, and overwhelmed by everything that was going on. And her feet still hurt. She sat down on the sofa, took off her shoes, and put on slippers. Yelling abruptly came from the girls' room. When the argument didn't stop, she got up and hurried down the hall.

"Put that down. It's mine," Morgan yelled at Dené.

"No, it's not. I brought this with me." Dené held a small, pink journal against her chest.

"No, you didn't. Sabre gave me that."

Morgan grabbed at the journal, but Dené turned away. Morgan reached around her and got her hand on the journal, trying to take it away. But Dené was taller and stronger. She spun again, making Morgan let go, then raised the journal in the air. Morgan jumped, trying to reach it, still yelling.

"Stop!" Sabre commanded, but they continued to shout and fight over the book. "That's enough!" This time, they both looked up at her. "Give it to me."

Dené hesitated, then handed her the journal.

"Now tell me what's going on."

They both started talking at the same time. Sabre held up her hand. "One at a time. Morgan, you first."

"Of course, she goes first," Dené said.

"It doesn't matter, you'll get your chance to tell your side." Sabre was exhausted and didn't want to deal with this right now. She was tempted to just take the journal and walk away, but she knew she had to resolve the issue between these girls. "Morgan?"

"You gave me that when I first moved in. You said I could use it for my daily word, or to write down my feelings, or whatever I wanted."

"Did you write anything in it?"

"No, because I put it away and forgot I had it. Dené must have found it." Morgan turned toward Dené. "Why were you going through my stuff, anyway?"

"I didn't touch your stupid stuff. That's my journal. My grandma gave it to me the last time I saw her. I even wrote in it when she gave it to me. Look, if you don't believe me."

Sabre opened the journal. The first page read: *September 1, from Grandma Goldie.*

"See," Dené said.

Morgan looked at the page. "She could've written that anytime. She probably did that so she could claim the journal." Morgan's face tightened with frustration. "It's mine. You know it's mine because you bought it for me."

"I bought one like it for you, but yours is a plain pink book. How about if I buy you another one?"

"That's not fair," Morgan shouted.

"Lots of things aren't fair," Sabre said. "But I'm doing the best I can here. I'll keep the journal until I can buy a second one." Both girls looked unhappy. "Why don't you go out in the backyard and cool off?"

Dené walked out without saying anything, and Morgan sat down on her bed, picking up a stuffed animal to hug.

"It'll work out," Sabre said.

"How can Dené not want to see her dad?" Morgan asked. "I'd give anything to see mine. She should be thankful he's around and not in prison. I just don't get it."

Sabre sat down on the bed next to Morgan. "It's different for you. You've had your father, at least off and on, all your life. He's been good to you, and you love him. Dené doesn't have that. Her father is a stranger to her, and I'm sure she'd love to have a relationship like you have with your dad. Please be patient with her."

Morgan sighed. "I'll try harder."

"Thanks, sweetheart." Sabre gave her a hug, then stood.

"I want my dad to come home."

Me too, Sabre thought, as she left the room. *I think.*

She went to her bedroom and changed clothes. Sabre didn't know how much more she could take. She needed a break, but she had to make dinner for the kids and get some work done on cases she'd been neglecting. What she really wanted to do was go somewhere quiet and just be alone for an hour, but she couldn't leave the girls because it was getting late. *Where was Conner?* He should've been home by now. She hoped JP would show up soon, but the last she'd heard, he was stuck in traffic.

Sabre went into the bathroom and splashed water on her face, hoping to feel more alert. Then she took a deep breath and headed toward the kitchen. She checked the refrigerator, trying to figure out what to make for dinner. Even that seemed like a huge task. She wasn't good at coming up with different meals, and she hated to cook. JP had been sharing the task, but lately it seemed to fall on her shoulders.

She realized she had what she needed for spaghetti. *Great.* She took out the hamburger, dumped it in a frying pan, then hacked at it with a wooden spoon to break it up.

Shouting started again from the girls' room.

Please stop.

When Sabre heard the front door open, she headed toward it, picking up her keys along the way. She met JP in the living room.

"Hi, sweetie," he said, kissing her lightly on the lips.

"Hi." She handed him the wooden spoon. "Conner isn't home. The girls are fighting. Hamburger is cooking on the stove for spaghetti, and I need a break." She walked out.

Once she started to drive, Sabre found herself headed in the direction of her condo. *Perfect. A quiet place with no one else around.* She hadn't been there in days. She had practically moved in with JP. It had just happened over time, ever since Morgan and Conner had come to live with them. Sometimes, she wasn't sure she was ready for that kind of commitment. It only worked for her because she kept telling herself it was temporary. In a few months, JP's brother, Gene, would be out of prison. She wasn't naïve enough to think he could take the children right away, or that he could even stay out of prison, but eventually, he might pull things together. Now, she had Dené, too. That was also supposed to be temporary, just until the girl and her dad could develop a relationship. But now Sabre had concerns about that after Dené's reaction at the birthday party. If the girls couldn't learn to get along, something had to change.

Sabre walked inside, got herself a glass of wine, which she seldom drank, and sat down on the sofa. She kicked off her shoes and just sat, letting her mind go blank. After several minutes, she took a sip of wine, then lay down. She pulled a throw blanket over her body and made herself comfortable. Within minutes, she was asleep.

She woke to the sound of her phone dinging. Sabre picked it up, noticing an hour had passed. The text was from JP.

JP: *Are you okay?*

Sabre: *I'm fine. I'm at my condo. I'll be home in a while.*

JP: *Take your time. Everything good here.*

Sabre was thankful to have JP in her life and felt guilty for her earlier thoughts. Everything would be okay. She would, no, *they* would get through all this.

Recalling Tara's suggestions for how to relax, she decided to try them out. After another sip of wine, she closed her eyes and took a deep breath through her nose. When she exhaled, she said "calm," then did the same with "relax and "in control." It seemed to work. She sat there listening to her own breathing, not thinking about anything, and letting her mind just enjoy the calm.

Suddenly, her eyes shot open, and a chill went through her body. She remembered something.

Chapter 39

Friday night

When Sabre walked in, JP stayed back, seeming hesitant to approach her until she reached out for him. He moved in quickly and wrapped his arms around her. They stood and embraced until Sabre finally let go.

"You okay?" JP asked.

She nodded and stepped back. "How are the kids?"

"They're good. Conner is out with some friends, and I think there's a girl with them that he's interested in."

"Why do you say that?"

"Because he asked if I had any cologne."

Sabre forced a smile. She was still shaking from her memory. "And the girls?"

"They're in bed, but probably not asleep. They're still a little angry at each other, but they haven't been yelling."

"I'd better go tell them goodnight."

Sabre went into their bedroom. The girls were as far apart in the bed as they could get, backs turned. Sabre tucked Morgan in and kissed her on the cheek. "Goodnight, Morgan."

"Goodnight," she mumbled.

Sabre walked around to the opposite side and said, "Goodnight, Dené." She got no response. Sabre bent down and kissed her lightly on the forehead.

"Thank you," Dené whispered.

Sabre rejoined JP in the living room. "I feel so sorry for that poor little girl."

"Dené?"

"Yes. And I hate that she and Morgan aren't getting along."

"Do you want to go to bed?" JP asked. "You look exhausted."

"No." Sabre sat down next to him. "I just want to sit here a bit and relax." She looked up at JP. "I remembered something tonight."

He took her hand. "Tell me."

"I was relaxing in my condo and suddenly, I felt very afraid. It was like I was back in the moment. I remember running in the parking lot, and I thought he caught me."

"Who?"

"I don't know, but I threw my shoe at him and ran. Then a car backed up and hit me. By the time I saw it coming, it was too late. But I was kind of numb, so I jumped up and kept running."

"Did you recognize the man?"

"No. The guy I threw the shoe at wasn't who I was afraid of. I'm sure of it. I thought maybe so at the time, but then I realized it wasn't him. Still, I kept running because I didn't know who he was. They could've been together."

"Can you see the person you were afraid of?"

"No, but I kept looking around for him. I think he was on foot because I wasn't looking for a vehicle. I was looking for a person, and I'm sure it was a man."

"Can you remember what happened next?"

"No, that's all I've got. The rest is totally blank until I woke up in the hospital."

"You don't remember the cops or the ambulance?"

"No, I'm sorry."

"Don't be. This is tough."

"I know, but it's odd. I want to know what happened, but it makes me feel so afraid. When I had the memory, everything flooded back, every feeling I had during those few minutes, and it's scary. Something worse happened earlier. I just know it. I mean, Harold was killed, and we don't know how. What if I killed him?"

"That's not likely, but if you did, you had a good reason."

Chapter 40

Chapter 40

Saturday morning

Travis arrived at the house to pick up Dené for their first outing.

"Hi Travis," JP said. "Come on in."

Travis usually seemed confident and comfortable around everyone, but today, he fidgeted with his keys as he waited for Dené.

"You're shakin' like a fifty-cent ladder," JP said. "Are you nervous?"

"A little. I know nothing about being a parent." Travis paced across the floor. "I know she likes animals, and she seemed a little excited about going to the zoo. I want her to have a good time, and I want her to like me, but I'm not sure we'll have anything to talk about. I'm never like this, but then I've never been in this situation before."

"You'll be fine. I went through a similar thing not long ago. I know it's not exactly the same, but I'd never raised kids, then suddenly, I had two looking to me for love and direction. You catch on quicker than you'd think."

When Dené, Morgan, and Sabre came into the living room, Travis stopped pacing and did his best to act calm. Dené, on the other hand, was obviously hesitant.

"Are you ready to go?" Travis asked.

"Can Morgan come along?" Dené blurted. "I'm sure she'd like the zoo, as well."

Morgan's eyes opened wide with surprise, and Dené gave her a pleading look.

"Of course," Travis said, sounding relieved. "If she wants to come, she's welcome."

Morgan stood there speechless for a few seconds, which was totally out of character for her. "Sure, I'd like to go. Give me a second. I'll grab a jacket." She dashed out of the room, and Dené followed her.

Travis sighed.

"I hope you don't mind Morgan tagging along," JP said. "But I have to warn you, she doesn't stop talking, so there won't be a dull moment." JP winked.

"Thanks," Travis said. "I think we'll all have a good day."

The girls hurried back, dashed out the door, and yelled goodbye as they left. Travis followed.

"That was strange," Sabre said. "Last night, the girls weren't talking to each other, and today they're off together."

"They're kids," JP said. His cell phone rang with a number he didn't recognize. "JP Torn," he said.

"This is Alex Griffin. Can you meet me at my home? I have something that might help us find Angela."

"Of course. Is right now okay?" He hung up.

"Who was that?" Sabre asked.

"The guy Powers told me about. He wants to meet with me."

"That's the guy who led you to Terry last time, right?"

"Yep."

"Hopefully he'll know something else worthwhile."

"I still don't understand why a respectable businessman like him is so involved with Xander."

"Didn't you say Powers thinks he's her john?"

"That's what doesn't fit. He seems so... *normal.* And he acted like he was genuinely concerned about her well-being."

"People can have unusual sexual behaviors and still seem relatively normal."

"I guess."

JP kissed her and left. On the way to his truck, his cell rang again. *DuBois.*

"You got time for a cup of coffee this morning?" the detective asked.

"Maybe later. I'm following up a lead on Angela."

"Anything you can share?"

"Not yet, but I will if I can." JP started his engine.

"By the way, I wanted you to know the flash drive didn't have anything important on it," DuBois said.

"What flash drive?"

"The one we picked up at Angela's house in the treasure box."

"I didn't know about that."

"That's right. You weren't there. Anyway, it was a dead end."

Chapter 41

Chapter 41

Saturday morning

Alex Griffin's home was a two-story stucco with oversized windows near Stevenson's Canyon. JP parked in the semi-circle driveway and strode to the tall double doors.

"Thanks for coming," Griffin said, inviting JP inside.

"No problem." JP looked around. "You have a beautiful home. I've always liked this area. Do you have a good view?"

"Come, I'll show you. I think it's spectacular."

They walked outside through the sliding glass door into the backyard, which was mostly stamped concrete. They passed a small guesthouse and stepped onto a huge deck that extended nearly to the edge of the property, which dropped off to a steep slope. Griffin's house sat in a curve, so he had a view on all three sides, with the ocean in the distance.

"Stunning," JP said. "Does someone live there?"

"No. I use it for storage."

They continued inside to the kitchen. "Can I get you something to drink? Soda maybe?"

"I'll have a Pepsi if you have one."

Griffin opened the refrigerator and looked inside. "I'm sorry, I thought I had some cold cans of Pepsi in here, but I guess I drank them all. There's soda in the garage, and I can pour it over ice."

"I'm good. Thank you."

"Sorry. Let's go to my office. I have something you might want to see."

They walked down a hall and into a corner office. Griffin offered JP a seat and sat down behind the desk, but didn't say anything.

JP leaned forward. "Do you know where Angela or Xander are?"

"No, but I found a last-known address for Angela's father."

"He was in Alabama. Is he local now?"

"Reggie Younger has never lived in Alabama. He has always been right here in San Diego."

"Wait a minute. I thought Angela's father was Frank Ormund. That's who's listed in DSS records."

"Xander put Frank's name down because she didn't want anyone to know who the real father was. And she knew Frank would not want any responsibility, leaving her to raise Angela alone, which was a better alternative."

"Did Frank know he wasn't the father?"

"I would assume so, since she never had sex with him."

"I don't understand," JP said. "Why didn't she name Younger? What's his story?"

"I'm only telling you this because Angela and Xander may be in trouble. I need you to keep it quiet. Younger is a horrible man, and if he figured out Xander's secret, he could be after her and the girl."

"I'll keep the secret if I can, but when it comes down to saving them, I'll get the job done, regardless."

"Fair enough," Griffin agreed. "I don't know how much you know about Xander's life as a child."

"Not much. Most of the information in the file is about her CPS history with Angela. I know she was adopted and her only relative is Jan Webb, who is the biological daughter of her adoptive parents."

"Yes, Jan was fifteen when her parents adopted Xander." Griffin picked up a manila file from his desk. "It's all in here, but I'll give you the short version." He took a breath. "Xander's parents were murdered in their home when she was a baby. Thank God she wasn't old enough to remember what happened. When Xander was four, her adoptive mother died of breast cancer. Her father continued to raise her, but he was pretty lost without his wife. He started drinking heavily and became a neglectful father. Xander had very little parental supervision, but in spite of that, she kept up her grades and took good care of herself."

"But she got pregnant at sixteen," JP said with no judgment.

"She was raped," Griffin spat.

"Reggie Younger?"

"Yes. He worked with her father and met Xander one day when she came to the office. After that, he started coming by the house and having drinks with her father. He introduced Xander to drugs, and shortly after, he raped her. Then he came back a few times and did it again, usually knocking her around. Xander was too afraid and ashamed to tell her father, so when she discovered she was pregnant, she left home and went to a shelter."

Griffin tapped the folder on the desk, took a deep breath, and went on. "Xander told me she cleaned up before Angela was born. She worked for a while in a fast-food place, but Angela was sick as a baby, and Xander lost her job because she missed too much work. She was a beautiful young woman and men wanted her. She discovered they were willing to pay for sex, and she could make a lot of money in a short time. But she couldn't handle it emotionally and started using drugs again. Eventually, it became a vicious circle for her, until she lost Angela the first time. You know the rest of the story."

"You have a current address for Reggie?" JP asked.

"It's in the file."

"Any criminal record for rape?"

"No. No record at all that my investigator could find. But he's definitely a predator. From what I can tell, he was named as a perpetrator in a juvenile dependency case, but I couldn't get that information. Maybe you can." Griffin handed the file to JP.

"Thank you for all of this. I'll see what I can do."

"Please don't confront him." Griffin stared at JP. "If he doesn't already know about Angela, that would certainly tip him off, possibly making both Angela's and Xander's lives a living hell."

"Okay, but I will have him tailed to see if we turn up anything. Don't worry, I'll be discreet." JP paused. "Why are you doing this for Xander?"

Griffin took a deep breath. "Because it's partly my fault she's on the street again."

JP gave him a puzzled look. "How is it your fault?"

"I told her something that upset her. Apparently, she couldn't handle it because shortly after that, she started using again."

"But you won't tell me what it is, will you?"

"No."

As JP left, he speculated about what could've upset Xander that much. *Did she ask for money and get turned down?* It had to be more than that. *Did Xander want to marry Griffin, and he rejected her? That seemed unlikely too.* But he would figure it out.

Chapter 42

Saturday afternoon

Reggie's house was located in Mission Hills, another nice area with a good view. Before driving over, JP ran the address on Zillow and discovered it was a three-bedroom, two-bath home worth one point three million. According to Griffin's file, Reggie had inherited it from his aunt, who died about five years ago.

JP parked across the street and a few houses down. There were no cars in the driveway, but the garage door was closed, so Reggie's vehicle could have been inside. JP checked the file again. Reggie's car was a nearly new Ford Mustang GT. The license plate number was listed too. Griffin had done his homework.

JP waited about ten minutes, then lost patience. He called Ron, Sabre's brother who'd worked for him many times, and asked if he could do surveillance. Ron showed up twenty minutes later, and JP left without talking to him, in case neighbors were watching. He'd given him all the information on the phone.

JP drove to the warehouse where Reggie worked as a manager. Ten years ago, he'd been a loan officer with Xander's father. The change of profession seemed odd.

The young woman at the front desk looked like a teenager. JP smiled as he approached, and she responded with a friendly hello.

"I'm looking for a guy named Reggie Younger."

Her face immediately lost its smile.

"Is he here today?"

"No," she said curtly.

"I get the feeling you're not fond of Reggie."

"I don't really know him. But, as I said, he's off today. Do you want to leave a message for him?"

"I don't really want him to know I was here." He decided she could be trusted. At least, he hoped so. "I'm a private investigator. My name is JP."

"I'm Georgia. And whatever it was, I'm sure Reggie did it."

She was so sweet, JP guessed she'd probably had trouble with Reggie's unwanted advances. She obviously wasn't impressed with him.

"Have you had a problem with Reggie hitting on you?"

Georgia looked surprised. "Yes, but why would you ask?"

"Because he seems to make a habit of hitting on young, attractive women."

"Thank you. He's just so...old and creepy."

JP couldn't help but smile. Reggie was not quite forty yet.

"I'm sorry. You must be as old as him." She sounded flustered. "Not that you're old-old. He's just so much older than me. Why would he think I'd be interested in him?"

"I know what you mean," JP said. "And I am *old*. But you're right, his behavior is uncalled for. Some men think they're God's gift to women. I have reason to believe he's one of them."

"He does it to all the young women around here. One recently quit because he wouldn't leave her alone. They were dating for a while, then suddenly a few days ago, she broke it off and quit, not wanting to be around him anymore. I don't know what happened, but I think it was big. I asked, but she wouldn't tell me. It's possible he dumped her, but I think it was more than that."

"Why, specifically?"

Georgia hesitated.

"You know something more," JP said. "Please tell me. It could be important."

Georgia sighed, then said, "She had a bruise on her cheek. She said she fell and hit her face on something, but I think it was Reggie. She denied it when I confronted her, but she seemed afraid of him."

"Has anyone reported him for his behavior?"

"Probably not. The boss wouldn't do anything about it. He needs Reggie."

"Would you mind giving me the name of the bruised woman who quit?"

"I don't think she'd want to talk about it."

"Look, Georgia, I understand you don't want to betray the confidence of a friend, but there's a lot at stake here. There may be an eight-year-old girl in danger because of Reggie. Don't misunderstand me. I'm not saying he's after the child, but he may be the key to finding her."

She was silent for a few seconds.

JP pressed further. "I'll keep your name out of it. No one will know where I got the information."

Without speaking, the girl pulled a sticky note off a pad and wrote *Holly Richards*, followed by a phone number. Georgia took a deep breath, then wrote something else on the paper and pushed it toward him.

"That's where she's working now. She went back to her old job and is there today."

JP thanked her, walked to his truck, and called Ron. "Any sign of Younger?" he asked.

"The garage door is opening as we speak."

"Is it him?"

"It's a red Mustang, but I'm not sure who the driver is." A pause. "Yup, that's him. He's pulling into the garage."

"Is he alone?"

"Yes. Unless someone is hiding in the car. He's getting out, and now the garage door is closing. The shades are drawn so I can't see anything in the house."

"Okay, thanks. Just stay there until you see some movement, or I call you."

"What if he doesn't come out again?"

"He will. It's Saturday. He'll be on the prowl." JP hesitated. "And, Ron, if you talk to Sabre, don't tell her where you are or who you're watching. Okay?"

"Why? Isn't this about the missing girl?"

"It is, but until I know more, I don't want her to have to disclose anything that might hurt her client."

Chapter 43

Saturday late afternoon

As JP pulled into the parking lot of the Found Hotel on Grape Street, his cell phone rang. *Sabre*. JP was vague about his location, saying only that he was "following up a lead." He hated holding things back from her, but if he told Sabre about Reggie, she would feel compelled to disclose the information to the court. Because Powers had given him Griffin's name in confidence, JP had avoided telling Sabre the specifics. He took a deep breath. He'd eventually disclose most of it, but not yet.

The lobby of the hotel was empty, except for the young woman behind the desk with the nametag that read *HOLLY*. She wore thick makeup, but it wasn't enough to cover the bruise on her cheek.

"Hi, Holly."

She looked puzzled and a little startled.

JP nodded toward her badge. "Your nametag."

"Sorry, I forget I'm wearing it. I'm not used to having my name on display." She smiled. "Are you looking for a room?"

"No, actually, I was looking for you."

She stiffened, dread in her eyes. "Why?"

"I'm a private detective, and I need to ask some questions about Reggie Younger."

Holly took a step back, then glanced around the lobby as if looking for a way out.

"Please, don't be scared. You have nothing to be afraid of."

She swallowed. "Did he send you to find me?" she asked in a meek voice.

"Nothing like that. As far as I can tell, Reggie is a real slime ball. I'm looking for him in relation to a missing child and her mother. It's possible he knows something about their disappearance."

"I wouldn't know anything about that."

"When did you last see him outside of work?"

"Wednesday night." She choked out the words, and tears filled her eyes. Holly clasped her hands, fingers intertwined, exposing white knuckles.

"Please don't be afraid. You don't need to tell me what happened because I can see how painful it is for you. But it might be of assistance to me if you can answer just a couple of questions."

She nodded.

"Did you go to his house on Wednesday?"

She nodded again, her fingers opening and closing nervously.

"Was there anyone else there? A woman or a young girl?"

She shook her head. "Not that I know of. I didn't see or hear anyone." Then, in a soft voice, "I wish I would have."

JP could only imagine what must've happened to her that night. Likely the same thing that happened to Xander when she was sixteen. JP felt a flash of rage. He couldn't stand men who hurt women or children, but what could he do? His inclination was to go punch the guy right now, but that wouldn't be of any benefit to Angela or Holly. "I don't know what Reggie did, but if you want, I can connect you with a nice police detective who may be able to help you."

She shook her head. "No, I just don't want to ever see or think of him again."

"Just one more thing. Do you know anything about what Reggie does when he's not working?"

"He brags about hanging out at a couple of local bars."

JP asked for the names. She told him, and he jotted them down on his notepad.

"I'm sorry for making you dredge up painful memories." JP left, knowing that was best for her, but he wasn't done with dear old Reggie. *He'd better give his heart to Jesus, 'cause his butt is mine.*

Chapter 44

Saturday night

As much as Sabre hated cooking, she took her turn when needed and made something simple. Tonight, it was chicken tacos. She was making dinner when Travis returned with the girls.

"Bye, Travis. Thank you," Dené said as she dashed to her room. Morgan said the same thing and followed her.

"They look happy," Sabre said. "How did it go?"

"Much better than I expected," Travis said. "Thanks for letting Morgan go along. She broke the tension. That girl sure can talk, and she uses all these big words, and correctly."

"Yeah, that's her thing."

"She's funny too."

"Yes, she is. Did the girls get along together okay?"

"Yeah, why?"

"They were having a tiff before they left," Sabre said. "They're still getting to know each other."

"Well, they seemed to have fun today. In fact, most of the time I could've just as well not been there, except to help them find things on the map."

"I'm sorry," Sabre said. "Maybe it wasn't such a good idea to send Morgan along. This is supposed to be your chance to bond with Dené."

"No. It was perfect. She needs to get comfortable around me. She has lost a lot, and she doesn't need a new parent forced on her. She'll come around."

Travis' concern for Dené impressed Sabre. At least she hoped that's what it was and not his own fear about the potential upheaval in his life.

Travis opened the front door to leave just as JP returned. "Did Morgan behave today?"

"She was great," Travis said. "That's quite a kid you have."

"Thanks. See you later." JP walked into the kitchen and hugged Sabre from behind. "Smells good in here."

"Call the kids and remind them to wash their hands. Dinner's ready."

They all sat down together and ate. The girls talked non-stop about the zoo and their favorite animals. Morgan liked the giraffes, and Dené's favorite was the okapi.

"The okapis are mine too," Sabre said. "They look so velvety, and they have fascinating markings, like they're part zebra."

"But they're not," Dené said. "They're in the same family as the giraffe."

"You're right, Dené. Our tastes must be genetic."

After dinner, JP said, "I need to take care of some business." He turned to the girls and instructed them to do the cleanup.

Conner smiled, Morgan moaned, and Dené said, "We'll do it."

Sabre walked JP to his truck. "Where are you going?"

"I need to check out a couple of bars."

"Is it Porter?"

"No, someone else, but he may be connected to Angela and Xander."

"The cops still haven't found Xander either?"

"No, and there's a chance they're together, but with Xander's background, she could be anywhere."

"You're being very evasive about this."

"Yes, I am."

"So, you won't tell me who you're following?"

"Nope."

"How do I know you're not seeing another woman?"

"Don't even pretend to be jealous. I know you, remember."

"You're right. I trust you," Sabre said playfully. "How about this approach? Did you forget who you're working for?"

"That's exactly why I can't tell you." He pulled her into his arms. "If I tell you what I know, you'll be compelled to provide the information to the court. I don't want you to do that until we know for sure. If this person knows something about Angela, it'll all come out anyway."

"So, when you leave can I expect my brother to show up?"

"Why would he do that?"

"I know you're tag teaming me. I expect Bob is in on it too. So, who will it be tonight?"

"No one, but if you see a police car drive by now and then, don't be alarmed." He kissed Sabre lightly on the lips.

Sabre smiled. "Go, find the girl."

~~~

JP drove downtown to one of the hangouts Holly had given him, the Star Bar. It was quite different from Porter's country tastes, which JP much preferred. Both were filled with obnoxious drunks and a lot of lonely people, but in this one, loud rock music blared.

JP had never seen Reggie, except for his Facebook photo, so it might be difficult finding him in a crowd later. For now, Reggie was still at home with Ron watching him.

He walked around, getting a feel for the layout, until his cell rang. JP stepped outside before he answered, so he could hear.

"Hi, Ron. Any change?"

"He just left, and I'm tailing him. He seems to be weaving his way out of Mission Hills."

"Any activity prior to this?"
~~~

"No, and I'm pretty sure he's alone. We just got on the 5 freeway, heading south."

"Keep the line open. He's probably headed downtown. My guess is the Gaslamp Quarter."

There was a brief silence. "How did you know that? We just got off the freeway, and we're headed south on Fourth."

"If he stops early, near E Street, he's probably going to the Star Bar. If he keeps driving, he's likely headed for the Werewolf. I got a little inside information."

"He's looking for parking." Ron was quiet again. "He's pulling into a parking garage on Fourth and F."

"He could go either way from there, but he's a little closer to Star Bar. Call me back as soon as you know which direction he's headed." JP stayed outside until his phone rang again.

"He's headed north on Fourth."

"Good. I'll wait just inside the door and join you when you walk in. Pass him if you can, then point him out when he comes in."

A few minutes later, Ron showed up and stood beside JP. "Reggie was right behind me, but he stopped to talk to a couple of women outside."

"I hope he doesn't take off with them."

"Nope," Ron said. "There he is."

JP watched the blond man stride up to the bar. Other than that he was muscular, he was very average looking—medium height, not particularly attractive, but nothing freaky about him either. JP turned to Ron. "Let's step out for a second. It's so loud in here, I can hardly hear."

Once outside, Ron asked, "What do you want me to do?"

"Stay here, keep an eye on him, and notify me immediately if he leaves."

"What's your plan?"

"I'll check to see if Angela is anywhere around his house."

"A break-in?"

"I'm just gonna look. Did you see any surveillance cameras or a Ring doorbell?"

"No. I looked it over pretty good with my binoculars, but I could've missed something. And who knows what he has inside. I did see him use the remote to close the garage door."

"That's good. Tell me exactly where he parked."

"Please don't do anything stupid."

"Come on," JP said, ignoring his comment. "We may not have much time, and there's a little girl missing."

Chapter 45

Chapter 45

Saturday night

With Ron's directions, Reggie's car was easy to find. JP kept the slim-jim tool under his shirt until he neared the Mustang. The parking garage had plenty of lights, but none were very bright. JP waited until a few cars and pedestrians cleared out, then wedged the slim-jim through the narrow gap at the top of the window. He pushed the thin metal strip down until the curved end reached the door-lock, then hooked it around the lever and jiggled. A few seconds later, the lock popped. A couple walked by just as he opened the door—with the slim-jim still in place.

JP froze and glanced over, but they were talking and didn't even notice him. No alarm had gone off, unless Reggie had a digital signal to his phone. JP reached in, checked the console, and removed the garage remote. He wiped down everything he had touched with a rag, left the door unlocked, and walked away.

It only took ten minutes to reach Reggie's house. A light was on in the front room, but JP didn't see movement. The garage was on the left side of the house, with bushes and a side yard about ten feet farther left. JP parked near the bushes so he wasn't in front of a neighbor's house and so his truck was close by if he had to leave quickly. Before he got out of his truck, a black sedan turned into the driveway right in front of him. JP waited until the couple went inside.

Ron hadn't called, so he figured he was safe, but he decided to check in anyway.

"Reggie's just drinking and hanging," Ron said. "Nothing unusual. Where are you, and are you okay?"

The music was so loud, JP could hardly hear him. "I'm fine. Just call me the minute he leaves."

"I will. But..."

JP couldn't hear the rest. Since Ron had started with 'But,' JP figured it was just a lecture. "I can't hear you. Talk to you later."

Another car passed, then JP got out and hurried toward the side of the garage. No motion lights came on, so he continued past the house. He wasn't visible to anyone on the street, so he would look around a bit before he opened the garage.

A window near the back of the house had no curtains or shades, but it was dark inside, and he couldn't see much. JP turned on his phone light and pressed it close to the glass. That helped a little, but all he could see was a bedroom with an empty bed. Time to go inside.

JP pushed the button for the garage door, and it started to open. He rounded the front corner and confidently walked inside, as if he belonged. He tapped his shoulder holster to make sure his gun was ready, then closed the door behind him. *Was that the right thing to do?* If someone was in the house, he could be in big trouble, but the closed door would keep neighbors from reporting or recording his moves.

He opened the interior door cautiously, wiped off the handle, and stepped into a hallway. JP moved quietly into the next room, a living space with lights on but no signs of life. Car magazines lay on the coffee table, along with a copy of Playboy. A pair of running shoes sat on the floor near an overstuffed chair, and a tablet lay near a partially filled coffee mug. Other than that, everything seemed in place.

The kitchen also had a light on, but it wasn't as neat as the living room. Dirty dishes sat on the counter and in the sink, and a crusty frying pan was on the stovetop. JP walked through without touching anything. He moved quickly and quietly, checking bathrooms and bedrooms for signs of anyone besides Reggie living there. He checked the closets in case someone was hiding, but found nothing.

When he reached an office/storage space, he noticed an attic entrance inside the closet. He pulled a chair in, climbed on it, and pushed the cover aside. He used his phone light to check around. The attic was filled with ducts and insulation, but a section was walled off. From his limited view, he couldn't see an opening. *Someone could be in there.*

JP remembered seeing a step stool in the pantry. So, he got down and retrieved the stool, which gave him just enough height to pull himself up into the attic. He kept his flashlight on and his gun handy as he approached the small room and finally saw the narrow door. He stepped inside—and recoiled.

JP holstered his weapon, then took photos of the chains, whips, spikes, and collars, along with various other *toys*. He shined his light across the room. There was a workout mat on the floor in the corner with a curly, blonde wig laying near the end. JP shuddered. *Could that be one of Angela's play wigs?* He took more photos, then climbed down.

Certain no one was in the house, he wiped off what he had touched, returned the step stool and chair to their original spots, and stepped into the backyard.

The small yard had no structures and very little landscaping. Weeds and dirt were the main attraction. Reggie obviously didn't spend much time there. JP didn't see any kind of security system or cameras, so he went through the fence gate and walked nonchalantly to his car. Two cars were coming toward him, but neither stopped.

Satisfied that neither Angela nor Xander were in the house right now, JP headed back downtown. When he called Ron, he didn't answer. JP figured he was still in the bar and couldn't hear the phone. He was confident Ron would call if Reggie left. Now all he had to do was put the remote back in Reggie's car, and the man would never know anyone was there, unless some nosey neighbor was spying on him.

JP was almost to the parking garage when his phone rang.

"He's leaving," Ron said.

"What direction?"

"Going north toward his car."

"Stay on the line. I'm just pulling into the parking lot, and I need to return something."

JP found a parking spot about six cars away from the Mustang, grabbed the remote, and got out.

"He's entering the garage," Ron warned.

"How close is he?"

Ron didn't answer. Instead, JP heard him say, "Excuse me. Is your name Reggie?"

"Yes. Do I know you?"

JP moved quickly toward the Mustang, still hearing the other men's conversation.

"We met a couple of years ago at the Werewolf," Ron said. "You were with some friends."

"Sorry, I don't remember you."

JP reached for the passenger door. He put the remote in, wiped the handle, and closed the door, just as Reggie and Ron came around the corner.

"Is that someone by my car?" Reggie asked as he came closer.

JP staggered away.

"Everything okay?" Ron asked.

"Yeah, he's probably drunk and couldn't find his car."

"The idiot," Ron said. "I'm getting out of here before he finds it and gets on the streets. Goodnight."

JP hurried back to his truck, and Ron called again. "That was close."

"Yeah. Good cover, by the way," JP said. "You can go home and get some sleep."

"Actually, I'm on my way to the Werewolf. I want to get there before he does."

"You don't need to. I think we found out what we needed." He told Ron about the room in the attic. "I got a chill when I saw the wig because I immediately thought of Angela playing dress up."

"Do you think it was hers?"

"It could be. We'll keep an eye on him in case Xander or Angela shows up there."

"Wow! That guy is a piece of work. I think I saw him slip something in a woman's drink, so I think I'll keep an eye on him a little longer tonight."

"But he didn't leave with anyone?"

"The woman ditched him and left the drink behind. Apparently, she wasn't impressed with him. But the next one might not be as selective."

"Be careful. Now that he's seen you, he'll be more tuned into your presence. Keep your distance."

Chapter 46

Sunday morning

JP was in the kitchen with Morgan, making breakfast, when Conner came in. The boy looked at JP and said, "Aiden and I want to ride our bikes to Torrey Pines Gliderport and watch the hang gliders and paragliders. Is that okay?"

"Sure. The food's ready, so sit down and eat first. You don't need to wait for the rest of us."

Conner was halfway through his meal when Sabre entered. When the boy told her his plans, JP heard the excitement in his voice. "I'd love to learn to parasail," Conner added. "But the equipment is very expensive."

"How much?" Sabre asked, as she made tea.

"The cheapest is around two thousand dollars."

"Yeah, that's not a cheap sport," JP said.

"If I get a job, I could save money and maybe buy one by this summer."

"I don't know about that," JP countered. "Your grades aren't that great, and if you're working, they may suffer more."

Conner looked disappointed.

JP offered an alternative. "You graduate in the spring. Maybe you could work over the summer to earn the money, then it won't interfere with school."

Conner shrugged. "Yeah, I guess."

Dené came in, said a lackluster "good morning," and sat down. Conner left shortly after, and JP put more pancakes and sausage on the table before sitting. He and Sabre chatted while they ate, but Morgan and Dené said little.

"Are you two fighting again?" Sabre finally asked.

"It's nothing," Morgan said.

'Yeah, it's nothing," Dené agreed.

"I need some relaxation time," Sabre said. "How about if we go to the beach? It's a nice day. We can walk around, go to the pier, maybe get an ice cream cone. What do you say?"

"I'm in," Morgan said.

"Me too," Dené added.

"How about you, JP?" Sabre asked.

"I'm at a dead end on these cases, so until something breaks, I can't do much. I think it's a great idea."

~~~

It was quiet at the beach. The tourists were mostly gone, and even though it was a Sunday, there were no crowds. This was Sabre's favorite time to go, when the locals could enjoy their ocean. At the water's edge, they walked in the sand. The girls took off their shoes and got their feet wet but jumped back quickly with the first wave.

"This was a good move," Sabre said.

"Yeah."

They strolled along the beach in silence, holding hands. For a few minutes, Sabre enjoyed the moment, taking in the salty smell of the ocean air, feeling the warmth of the sun on her back, and hearing the waves crash beside her.

Suddenly, darkness flooded her mind and her chest tightened. She squeezed JP's hand.

"What's the matter?" he asked.

Searing pain now. Sabre wrapped her hands around the top of her head.

JP put his hands on her shoulders. "Tell me what's wrong!"

"My head hurts." Her breath felt heavy.

JP grabbed his phone. "I'm calling an ambulance."
~~~

"No," Sabre said, catching her breath. "I'm just scared." She let out a short, loud gasp. "I remember... someone is beating... Harold." More short breaths as memories flooded her. She recalled what the hypnotist had told her. Sabre took a deep breath through her nose and let it out of her mouth, saying "Calm" at the same time. She did the same with *relax* and *in control*, then took another deep breath and looked around. "Where are the girls?"

"They're fine. I can see them." JP turned back. "Are you sure you don't need a doctor?"

"I'm okay." *Mostly*. The images had been terrifying. "I saw someone beating Harold. I tried to stop him, but the man kicked me and I fell down. I heard Harold yelling, 'Run! Run!' So, I did."

"Can you see who the man is?"

Sabre shook her head. "I can't see his face."

Chapter 47

Monday morning

The Eddie Blane case

Sabre waited in the conference room at Voices for Children, the San Diego chapter of CASA, for her appointment. She was fifteen minutes early, so she spent the time reading through the Blane file. A man opened the door and stepped inside. He had thick, white, wavy hair, soft brown eyes, and a white, trimmed mustache. The CASA volunteer shifted the laptop he was carrying to his left hand and extended his right.

"Dr. Mark Upton," he said with a friendly smile. "It's a pleasure to meet you."

"You as well."

Sabre was impressed that he was early and pleased with the way he was dressed. He either took the job seriously, or had just come from another appointment because his tall, lean body was clad in a sports jacket and slacks. He moved with an air of confidence.

Once seated, he immediately started talking about the case. "I've made a timeline of the illnesses Eddie's had based on the medical records. The chart includes the symptoms and the treatment. Office visits are in yellow, and hospitalizations are in blue. I spoke to the mother at length, with her attorney present, as well as other friends and family, and I've added their accounts of sicknesses that weren't treated professionally. Those are in green." He opened his laptop. "I can explain it better if you look at the spreadsheet."

Once he had the timeline on the screen, he began to explain. "This child has been hospitalized sixteen times and has had over sixty visits to doctors, including urgent care and ER visits when he wasn't hospitalized. The mother has changed doctors several times." He scrolled through the spreadsheet and counted. "Eddie has had seven primary care doctors, plus all the ones in the hospital and clinics. All in all, he has been seen by approximately a hundred different medical professionals."

"That's a lot of doctors for such a short period of time." *You'd think one would've figured out if there was something seriously wrong with the child.* Sabre kept her thoughts to herself. She didn't want to influence the doctor in any way.

"It wasn't until the last hospital visit that the child was reported to CPS, although there were a couple of times when his illness was questioned." He pointed at the spreadsheet again. "There were comments in the record that indicated some doubt."

"What do you think, doctor?"

"I haven't examined Eddie, although I've spoken to him several times. I'm not ready to say this is Factitious Disorder, nor am I ready to say this child is chronically ill. He does have a few serious allergies and asthma. There's no question about that. But there is no evidence of poisoning or anything of that sort. He possibly had an issue with mold, but that was resolved, and any further mold contact has been ruled out."

"Have you observed him with his mother?"

"I have. She appears very loving with him, but that's not unusual in either scenario. I've encountered a few cases during my practice that were possibly Factitious Disorder. One was with a child, the other with an aging parent. I'm not certain if either was valid, but I researched the subject at the time. The offender always shows a great deal of attention to the victim and, in fact, loves the victim. They just have an even greater need for the attention the illness brings on themselves." He paused. "Has the mother had a psychological evaluation?"

"The court can't order a psych until after it takes jurisdiction," Sabre explained. "It can then be used for dispositional purposes."

"I don't understand. If the basis for this petition is the mother's mental health, wouldn't it be an important factor?"

"It would, but the department has made certain allegations that social workers say they can prove. They can't order the defendant to do something that might help prove *their* case. That would be bootstrapping. They either have the evidence, or they don't. They can't compel the defendant to provide it for them."

"I guess that makes sense."

"Eddie said his mother gave him 'special medicine,'" Sabre said. "He had no idea what it was. He said sometimes it made him feel better and other times it made him worse. Are you concerned about what she was giving him?"

"Absolutely. The mother claimed it was various homeopathic remedies, which I'm not personally opposed to. Lots of cultures have used them for thousands of years, and they work for certain things."

"But you sound hesitant."

Dr. Upton took a deep breath. "The mother gave me bottles of what she had given him and mentioned other concoctions she'd found on the internet. All of which sounded harmless, unless he had an allergic reaction. The real problem is we don't know what she *really* gave him. We know what she *said* she gave him, but if she is the one making him sick, she's probably lying about the meds, too."

"When will you examine Eddie?"

"I plan to do it this afternoon. The social worker has given me permission." He met her eyes. "You're his attorney. Are you okay with that?"

"Yes, I've already approved it."

"Good. In the meantime, I've got a call into a couple of colleagues who might be able to guide me. One is a pulmonary specialist, and the other is a psychiatrist. Hopefully, they can give me some insight. I called the cardiologist because Eddie's symptoms often include low blood pressure and rapid heart rate."

"I'm impressed, Dr. Upton. You certainly are thorough."

"Please call me Mark. And thank you. Eddie deserves to be appropriately diagnosed. He either needs better treatment or a better home life. He seems to be doing fine in his aunt's home, but it's only been a few days. And that also seems to happen when he first goes home to the mother. Maybe that's because Eddie believes he should be better. Maybe it's because his mother allows him to be better. Or maybe it's because his symptoms have been treated. We need more time to determine that." The doctor scowled. "It is bothersome that when the mother visited yesterday, Eddie took a turn for the worse."

"But the visit was supervised, correct?"

"Yes. She couldn't have given him anything that would have triggered it. Both the aunt and I closely watched her, and she was never left alone with him."

"Did she say anything that was inappropriate?"

"No, but she's had eight years to condition the child. Her presence alone might set him off."

Chapter 48

Monday afternoon

Detective DuBois met with Sabre and JP at a quiet coffee shop in a central location.

"JP said you remembered something else," the detective said. "I hate to put you through this, but I need anything you can tell us."

"I know," Sabre said. "I'm doing better with it now. At first, I felt intense anxiety and fear. But I've mulled it over in my mind and although it's frightening, I'm accepting that it's just a memory. The worst is over."

"Please tell me exactly what you recall."

"I don't know how I got there, but I was in the canyon where Harold was found. Someone had just pulled me out of the car. I know I was struggling, but I can't tell why or with whom. Then it gets foggy. At some point I heard Harold ask if I was okay to walk, and I said yes. I don't know what happened next, but suddenly a man was hitting Harold. I don't know where he came from or if he's the one who pulled me out of the car."

"Can you see his face?"

"I should be able to, but it's blurry to me."

"What about his hair or skin color?" DuBois asked. "Was he light or dark?"

"I'm not sure." Sabre took a deep breath. "I saw his hand go up in the air, holding a pistol, then he came down hard with it. I screamed and Harold jerked, but he still took the blow on his shoulder. Harold stumbled, and the man came toward him, still gripping the gun. But this time, he was aiming it at his chest. I screamed for him to stop, but he wouldn't, so I ran at him from behind. He swung around and flung me to the ground." Sabre swung her arm to demonstrate. "I hit the dirt pretty hard."

"You used your right hand. Is that what he did?"

Sabre thought for a moment. "I think so."

"Did he still have the gun?"

"Yes, it was in his left hand."

"Which hand was he using when he hit Harold?"

Sabre studied her memory. "His left hand. Yes, I'm sure of it."

"When the man came at you and his hand reached out to strike, did you see what color it was?"

"It was white. And I saw it when he hit Harold. Definitely white."

"That tells us he's a white man who is likely left-handed." DuBois made a note. "What happened after he hit you?"

"I see him holding a gun real close to my face. All of a sudden, I see Harold hitting the man on the head with a rock, but he couldn't get a good strike, and it didn't faze him. Harold kept yelling for me to run, but I couldn't seem to move. The next thing I know is that the man is pounding on Harold." Sabre choked back tears. "I must have left him there to die."

JP wrapped an arm around her and pulled her close. "You did the right thing."

"It doesn't feel like it," Sabre sobbed.

"You tried to stop him, but you couldn't. If you hadn't run, he would've killed you too. Then you'd both be dead." JP's voice softened. "I'm really sorry Harold died. He certainly appeared to be trying to help you. But selfishly, I'm just glad you're alive."

"JP is right, you know," DuBois said. "If someone comes at you with a gun, chances are, their intent is to kill you."

"I suppose."

"Can you continue with this?" DuBois asked.

Sabre swallowed and took a deep breath. "I'm okay. Let's do it."

"Did the man say anything?" DuBois asked.

"He did, but I can't remember the words, although I think there was something familiar about his voice. In my brain, the words are all distorted. It sounds like Dory speaking whale."

"What?" JP asked, looking at her quizzically.

"Dory thinks she's speaking whale, and her words are difficult to understand," DuBois explained.

"Exactly," Sabre said.

JP tipped his head and glanced from one to the other. "You're both weird." He focused on DuBois. "How do *you* know what she's talking about?"

"From the movie, *Finding Nemo*."

"Finding Nemo?"

"Yes. I have kids and grandkids, and I've fallen asleep to that movie many times." DuBois cleared his throat and, using whale speak, said, "It sounds like this."

Sabre couldn't help but smile. JP just shook his head.

"Is there anything else you can remember about the perp?" DuBois asked. "Was he tall or short?"

"He seemed like a giant when he came at me, but my mental image when he approached Harold from behind is different. He was a little taller than Harold and muscular."

"Did he have facial hair?"

"I can't see his face well enough to say."

"How about scars or tattoos?"

"I think he had a tattoo on his right arm, but I'm not sure. All I recall is something red. I can't get a visual of it, so it may have been blood because he had already hit Harold several times."

"Can you think of anything else?"

"No, I'm sorry."

"You've given me a lot, and now that those memories have returned, you'll likely get more."

"I hope so."

Chapter 49

Chapter 49

Monday night

Sabre and JP sat outside on the patio, rehashing the interview with DuBois and speculating about how the new information applied to their suspects.

"Do you know if Lynch is right- or left-handed?" JP asked.

Sabre thought about the times she'd seen Lynch and tried to recall if she ever saw him write anything. "When he pinned me that time in my office, he slammed his left hand hard against the wall. So it could be his dominant hand, or maybe he wanted his right hand free. I can't remember seeing him sign anything."

"What about the Holloways?" JP asked.

"Waylon is left-handed, but we know it wasn't him since he was in custody. I've never seen Porter, and I only saw Gunner twice, and that was in court, and I was busy. You've been around Porter a couple of times, and you saw Gunner up close. Do you remember?"

JP thought for a second. "Porter shot pool with his right hand. That's certain. And when I saw him at the construction site, he used his right hand to drill screws. As for Gunner, the only thing I can remember is a gesture where he ran his hand through his hair, and he used his left hand. I'm not sure that counts for much."

"True."

"DuBois called a bit ago and told me they found a shell casing of a 45 caliber near where Harold was killed. According to the medical examiner that matched the size of the wound. So, we're looking for a 45 caliber semi-automatic handgun. DuBois also said the ME believed even without the gunshot, he would have likely died from the beating he took. He was pretty torn up."

"But we can't connect the gun to anyone, so how does it help? No judge will issue a search warrant on the flimsy evidence we have for Lynch or the Holloways. And what are the chances that the perp kept the weapon anyway? It was probably stolen, and now it's likely in a trash bin somewhere or at the bottom of the ocean." Sabre took a breath. "No. The killer is most likely a complete stranger. If not, why wouldn't he still be coming after me? No one knows I lost my memory except the few people working the case. So, the perp would think I could identify him."

"Don't think I haven't thought about that."

"Which is why you've been sticking so close, or Ron has been hanging around."

"I know how you hate that, so I've been trying not to smother you. But I worry when you're not in my sight."

When Sabre's cell phone rang, she glanced at the name. "I have to take this. It's the Munchausen case."

JP stood and went inside.

"Hello, Dr. Upton."

"I saw Eddie today." He jumped in without any small talk. "I gave him a thorough examination. I'm also looking at the blood sample taken this morning, and I spoke to a pulmonary doctor. He's agreed to meet with me and two other specialists tomorrow morning."

"That's great."

"If I were practicing in a hospital, we'd work as a team, which is much more effective on tough cases. In the meantime, I think we've ruled out myalgic encephalomyelitis/chronic fatigue syndrome. I know you had some concern about that."

"My concern was not specifically with that disease, but with any condition that isn't likely to be detected."

"And that was a good point. As for ME/CFS, it seldom affects children as young as Eddie, and it's more often present in women than men. Although Eddie is tired a lot, he doesn't have the extreme fatigue that manifests in ME/CFS, and he doesn't have the sensitivity to pain or the swollen joints that would surely be evident."

~~~

Once outside of Sabre's earshot, JP called Ron.

"What can I do for you?"

"Any chance Reggie is a lefty?" JP asked.

"I should know that?" Ron responded with a question, as he often did.

"You watched him for an hour at the first bar and another two hours at the Werewolf. Did you notice which hand he held his drink in? Did he sign a credit card receipt? Did he pull a chair out for a woman to sit down? Anything?"

"I know those are all things *you* would notice. I'm trying to run them through my mind, but I can't recall a pattern. I think his drink was mostly in his right hand, but when he spiked that woman's drink, I think he used his left hand. I'm sorry, JP. I should've been more attentive. Maybe I'd better stick to my day job."

"You don't need to apologize. You did a great job keeping an eye on him. Hopefully, it'll lead to something that puts Reggie away for a while."
~~~

Chapter 50

Tuesday morning

The sun had just come up, and Sabre put on her running shoes and left the house. It had been a while since she'd gone for a morning run, and she needed it. Her feet were finally healed enough to handle the pounding. She would stay in the neighborhood on a route she'd taken many times and watch for any strange activity.

Sabre told herself to breathe, not think about work, or her incident, or anything unpleasant. The hardest concern to keep down was Angela's disappearance. Sabre picked up her pace. It wasn't long before she was in the zone, enjoying the run, and ignoring everything around her. It felt good to let the endorphins flow. She kept herself in the moment, not thinking about all the problems in her life.

Suddenly, a blue Ford pickup pulled over to the curb just ahead of her. Sabre froze, and fear filled every inch of her body as memories surfaced. She reached into her pocket, pulled out her phone, and tapped JP's icon.

"Where are you?" he asked. "You know I don't like you to go out by yourself this early."

"I... I'm..." Sabre took a step backward as the door of the truck opened.

"Sabre," JP said. "What's wrong?"

A man got out of the truck and headed in her direction. He was short, brown-skinned, and white-haired.

"It's not him." She sighed with relief.

"Not who? What's wrong?"

"I... I'm okay. I went for a run, then I remembered seeing a blue truck, but not where Harold was killed."

"Where are you? I'm coming to get you."

"I can run back. It's not that far."

"No, I'm coming. Stay on the phone with me."

Sabre told him the street name, then turned and headed back. JP continued to talk to her until they met a few blocks away.

"Dang it," JP said as she got into his truck. Sabre was silent, and he said in a softer voice, "Please don't do that again. I know you hate feeling like a victim, but this is a real threat. You witnessed a murder. If you weren't the target initially, you could be now. The perpetrator might be looking for you, and if he knows you, he could know your daily patterns. Please."

"Okay. But the run opened up my brain. I remember seeing a truck and the license plate, but I can't remember the number."

"How do you know you saw the plate?"

"I studied it, just briefly, but it didn't stick. And the truck wasn't in the canyon. It was by Angela's house, but I'm sure it's related because I felt the same fear. And the man was wearing a mask, like for COVID. That's why I can't see his face, but even the rest of his face is blurry to me."

"But you're sure it wasn't the same man who just got out of the truck back there?"

"Yes, I'm sure. He was short, round, and sixty-something. The perp is taller, muscular, and younger."

JP pulled away from the curb. "Are you okay, really?"

"My feet hurt."

~~~

Juvenile court was crowded with a lot of new cases from the weekend. Since the DA's office had seventy-two hours to set the arraignments and the detention hearings, Wednes-
~~~

days were always a busy day. Sabre wound her way through the mob until she met Bob in the lounge.

"Did you see the supplemental report on the Blane case?" Bob asked.

"Yes. I picked it up earlier."

"The social worker is really going after the mother. She has half a dozen people who are voicing their opinion about how the mother made Eddie sick. How do they know? They're not medical professionals. And Eddie's father, of course, is blaming his ex. He hasn't even been involved in the case, but apparently, he doesn't like my client much." Bob continued to rant. "Willow said Eddie's dad is a real loser, a womanizer who can't keep a job and seldom pays support. The county has gone after him, but once they garnish his wages, he quits his job."

"Are you done?" Sabre asked.

"No. The aunt blames the mother too. Think about that. Willow knows her sister blames her, but she still wanted Eddie with Klara rather than foster care because she thought it was best for him. Doesn't that show her love for her son?"

"No one doubts that she loves him. If she has Factitious Disorder, then she has her own issues that are stronger than her love for her son."

"But if her son is really sick, it's not her fault."

"And that's why we're trying to sort it out," Sabre said. "Bob, I can see how passionate you are about this case. You apparently believe your client, and that's a good thing. You'll fight hard for her, but I'm going to fight for Eddie as well."

"You think Mom is making him sick?"

"I don't know yet. Dr. Upton is doing all he can to determine if this child is sick. He's put together a team of doctors to look at Eddie's symptoms and make a determination. But if they can't come up with anything, and Eddie's other doctors come to the same conclusion, the blame will fall back on the mother."

"Doctors aren't infallible. Just because they can't diagnose him doesn't mean he isn't sick."

"Or maybe they can't find anything because there's nothing to find."

"So, you've made up your mind." Bob sounded angry.

"No, I haven't," Sabre protested. "I'm doing my best to look at all the evidence and keep an open mind." Sabre sighed. "This isn't like you. Why are you getting so angry?"

"Because I believe my client. If you could hear the concern she has for her child you might think differently. She's had a hard time. Her ex-husband is an ass, her family gave up on her, and she's had to deal with a sick child for most of his life. She's counting on me to help her finally get the right diagnosis and medical attention for her child. She's exhausted, and scared, and angry at the system and the doctors."

"And if it turns out she's the one with the disorder?"

"Then you know I'd want that child protected. But unless they actually diagnose what is wrong with Eddie, we won't ever really know if it's the mother who is ill, or the doctors who don't know enough about medicine."

"I know you don't want to see that little boy suffer any more than I do." Sabre hated when she and Bob didn't see eye to eye. But this was unlike him. He always fought hard for his clients, but he must believe her or he wouldn't be so invested.

"I'm sorry, Sobs. I shouldn't take this out on you. I know you'll be fair. I'm just so frustrated."

Chapter 51

Tuesday night

Sabre sat quietly on a bench swing in the backyard. She was deep in thought when JP joined her carrying a can of beer. Neither spoke at first, but Sabre gave him a skeptical look. JP put his arm around her and pulled her close.

"Let's forget about everything for a little while and just enjoy each other's company," Sabre said.

"A great idea." JP let go and popped open the beer.

"When did you start drinking Bud Light?" Sabre asked.

"It was left over from your birthday party. I thought I'd give it a try."

Sabre gave him a curious look, but said nothing else. They talked about the beautiful sky and the flower garden, but the serenity didn't last long. Their conversation quickly turned to the kids and then to the missing girl.

"Anything new on Angela?" JP asked.

"No," Sabre said. "She's been gone a week, and so has her mother. I have to think they're together, but I can't even imagine where. Do you think there's a chance Xander cleaned up and went somewhere with Angela so CPS wouldn't take her away again?"

"I wish that were true, but I don't think Xander cleaned up overnight. According to a witness, she was in bad shape shortly before Angela disappeared."

"A witness? Who's the witness?"

"I'd rather not say right now. Besides, Xander's been in the system before. She knows if she gets clean, she gets her kid back. I'm not saying they aren't together, but I doubt it's because Xander cleaned up her act."

"Which means either someone has them both, or Xander is hiding Angela somewhere that's unsafe for a child."

"Exactly. I followed up on a couple of potential leads, but they were dead ends. I'm at a loss as to what to do next." JP sounded frustrated.

Sabre felt that way too. "I so hoped DuBois would've found something helpful in Angela's room, like maybe the flash drive."

"What's with that? DuBois mentioned it, but he said it didn't lead them anywhere. He thought it might have some information on the drive that would help them, but I guess there wasn't anything important."

"The flash drive was in her treasure box, so it probably had some significance to Angela." Sabre recalled another detail. "Her aunt said it used to have three keys on it, but when DuBois found it, there was only a skeleton key."

"And they haven't found anything the skeleton key fits?"

"No, but it's likely Angela just picked it up somewhere. Jan has been looking for the other two keys, but they're gone."

"Do you think Angela might have them with her?"

"Maybe, but we have no idea what they're for, so it doesn't really matter.

"So the flash drive was a keychain . . ."

"And an airplane."

JP turned to stare at her. "What kind of plane?"

"A little jet with Boeing printed on the side."

"Boeing?" JP almost shouted.

"Yes. DuBois checked it out, and Boeing gave away thousands of those. Anyone could have one."

"You're sure it was Boeing?"

"Yes, I'm sure," Sabre said. "What's with you?"

JP stood and grabbed his jacket. "I have to go. I have a hunch."

"About where Angela is?"

"Yes."

"I'm going with you." Sabre followed him inside. He grabbed his keys and stepped toward the front door.

JP hesitated, then said, "Okay. If this pans out, you need to know anyway." He stopped. "Wait. What about the girls?"

"They're in bed. It's a school night."

"I didn't realize it was that late."

"Me either," Sabre said. "I'll tell Conner we're leaving and ask him to keep an eye on them."

"Get your jacket. It's getting chilly."

Within minutes, they were in the truck and on their way.

"Where are we going?" Sabre asked.

"I got the name of one of Xander's johns from her attorney, and he made me promise not to tell anyone. I checked the guy out and couldn't find any reason to think he was involved with the disappearance. However, he led me to someone else who seemed like a possible suspect, but so far, he hasn't panned out either."

"You're talking in circles. Why can't you tell me their names?"

"Because the second guy is someone you'll have to disclose to the court if you know about him. And the consequences for Xander and Angela could be devastating."

"I'm totally confused. And you haven't answered my original question. Where are we going?"

"To see Xander's john."

Sabre put it together. "Oh, that's the guy you mentioned before, but wouldn't give me full information about."

"Right."

"So, why now?"

"Because he's a big deal at Boeing."

"Whoa. I didn't see that coming."

JP drove west on Balboa and turned right toward Stevenson's Canyon.

"The guy seems so normal and nice," JP said. "It's hard to imagine he hooked up with Xander. Although, he did say she was quite different when she was clean."

"They usually are. And Xander is very attractive. When she's cleaned up, she can hold her own with the best of them."

"Griffin, that's the guy's last name, is a good-looking man as well, and very personable. It's hard to imagine he pays for sex."

"Do you know for a fact that he's her john?"

"I only know what Powers told me, and that's how he described him. But maybe he just made that assumption."

Ten or fifteen minutes later, JP parked in front of Griffin's house.

Sabre had a moment of alarm. "Do you think he kidnapped Xander and Angela?"

"Let's go find out."

"If he did, he's not just going to admit it. What if he's dangerous? Should we call DuBois?"

"No, but maybe you should wait in the truck."

"Not a chance."

Chapter 52

Chapter 52

Tuesday night

JP rang the bell, and it was only a few seconds before Griffin answered the door. "JP, what are you doing here? Did you find Angela and Xander?"

"No. I hope you don't mind, but I have an idea where Angela is." JP turned to Sabre. "This is her attorney, Sabre Brown."

"Yes, I recognized her. Hi, Sabre."

"Have we met before?"

"No, but I've been to court with Xander a few times. I never went inside the courtroom, but Xander pointed you out in the lobby." He pushed the door open wider. "Come on in."

JP and Sabre walked into the meticulous living room.

"Nice home," Sabre said.

"Thanks, have a seat." Griffin picked up the remote control, shut off the television, then started to sit down. When JP and Sabre remained standing, so did he.

"Have you heard from them?"

"No," Sabre said. "But Angela is very clever, and she probably sees this as some great adventure."

"Do you think she's living out on the streets at night? With her mother, maybe?" He sounded worried.

"I suppose that's possible," JP said. "Maybe they've found shelter somewhere different from Xander's usual hangouts."

"Have you been back to Terry's?" Griffin asked. "Maybe they're staying there."

"I don't think so." JP thought Griffin sounded sincere. He hoped so. He was beginning to like the guy.

"So, where are they?" Griffin asked. When JP didn't respond right away, he asked again. "You said you had an idea where the girls are. What do you know?"

"Let me ask you a couple of things first," JP said.

"Okay."

"Did you give Angela a flash-drive keychain shaped like an airplane?"

"Yeah, about six months ago."

"Did it have keys to your house on it?"

"Yes," he said slowly. "Why?" His tone changed to defensive. "Do you think I'm hiding them? I wouldn't do that."

JP raised a palm. "No, I don't. Just stick with me here."

"Okay." Griffin sighed, but still looked impatient.

"I have a pretty good idea of where they are," JP said. "Angela had two keys, and..."

Before JP could finish, Griffin grabbed his keys and headed out the back door. JP and Sabre stayed close behind.

"She has a key to the guest house," Griffin said.

"Have you been in it lately?"

"Not in months."

JP had a hunch Angela was here on her own, but if Griffin had them locked up, they would find out soon enough. "When I was here last time, you thought you had Pepsi in the fridge, but it wasn't there. Has anything else gone missing?"

"Milk, bread, and cereal seem to be going fast." Griffin shook his head. "Do you think Angela has been in my house taking food?"

"Angela took the keys when she left her Aunt Jan's house. I think it's because she knew she could come here and be safe."

"I told her she was always welcome. That was at a time when Xander's behavior was changing, and I didn't want to accuse her, but I was concerned she was using again. As it turned out, she was. So, I gave the keys to Angela and told her if she was ever in a bad situation to come here. She has my number, but not her own phone."

When they reached the guest house, Griffin unlocked it, and they heard scrambling.

JP stepped forward. "Let me go first. There could be someone else in there. What is the layout?"

"It's basically a studio. The only other room is the bathroom."

JP pulled out his gun and carefully stepped inside. Nothing moved. He flipped the light on and glanced around. No one was there. A Pepsi can and a partially eaten bowl of popcorn sat on the bar in the kitchen area, and the sofa bed was extended. JP opened the closet and looked inside. It was packed full of containers. Then he moved across the room to the bathroom door. He tried to turn the handle, but it was locked.

"Angela," JP called.

No answer, and no sound coming from the bathroom.

"Angela, it's JP, your attorney's investigator. Do you remember me?"

Still nothing.

Griffin had come inside, and JP turned to him. "Do you have a key for the bathroom?"

"I'll be right back."

JP stepped closer to the door, but stood back so he wasn't directly in front of it. He wasn't taking any chances in case he'd called this wrong. "Angela, we're getting a key. You might as well open the door. No one wants to hurt you. You'll be safe."

JP waited. A few seconds later, he heard the handle click, and the door opened. Angela walked out, followed by her mother.

Chapter 53

Chapter 53

Tuesday night

Sabre embraced Angela, so relieved the girl was safe. But she looked tired, and her clothes were stained from a week's wear. "Are you all right?"

"I'm fine, just a little hungry."

"What in the world?" Griffin said. "Why didn't you just ask me for help?"

"This is all my fault," Xander said.

"No, Mom, it's mine."

Everyone was talking at once, so JP called out, "Stop!"

It got quiet for a second, then Sabre turned to Griffin. "Can we all go back to the main house, get them something to eat, and talk about this?"

"Absolutely."

They gathered around the island bar in the kitchen, most on barstools, except Griffin, who stood in front of the open pantry.

"You have a lot of food there," Sabre said.

"Yeah, that's why it's not that noticeable when something goes missing. The Pepsi has been the most obvious."

"That's your favorite, right Angela?" JP asked.

"Yes," Angela said. "How did you know?"

"I remember your aunt telling us that. That's part of what triggered my curiosity."

"Every day I seemed to be short a can or two from the refrigerator, but I also thought I had more in the garage." Griffin continued to look in the pantry. "I'm sure I had a large can of nuts, and my soup seems to be depleted, and my peanut butter has gone down pretty fast. How am I doing Xander?"

"Angela did a good job of keeping us fed," Xander said, and looked at Angela.

"I never took too much of anything at one time. And I tried to clean up after myself so you wouldn't notice. I'm sorry we ate your food."

"Don't you be sorry about eating anything I have, but you should have just told me."

When Angela looked down at the floor, Griffin stepped over by her and gave her a quick squeeze. "I'm just glad you didn't go hungry. Speaking of which, I can make roast beef sandwiches quickly, if that works for everyone."

"JP and I have already eaten, but thank you."

"I like roast beef," Angela said.

"While you're cooking, I'll take Angela in another room to talk," Sabre said. "JP, please get Xander's version of what happened, then we'll figure out where we go from here."

"Consider it done," JP said.

"You can use my office," Griffin offered. "It's just down the hallway."

"Let's go, Angela." Sabre needed to hear the girl's thoughts without her mother present. Angela followed her, and they sat down in comfortable leather office chairs.

"You had a lot of people worried about you," Sabre said.

"I'm sorry. I didn't mean to upset anyone. I just wanted to help my mom."

"I know, and I'm glad you're safe. But you need to tell me exactly what happened."

The girl sighed. "Mom was waiting for me when Aunt Jan dropped me off at school. She had called me the night before and said she wanted to get clean and be my mother again. So, I told her to meet me at school and I'd help her. I didn't know if she would actually show up." Angela shrugged. "Sometimes, she says things like that and doesn't really mean them."

"But this time she was there?"

"Yes. She was waiting near a tree and called me over when I got out of the car."

"So, you never went inside?"

"No. She said we couldn't talk at the school because they'd chase her away, so we walked down the street to the park. She said she really wanted to get sober, and I told her about my plan."

"Your plan was to come here?"

"It seemed like the best thing. I had keys to Alex's house and the apartment out back. He'd let me use it as a playhouse sometimes for my adventures."

"How did you get here?"

"I had a few dollars, so we took a bus. But we didn't have enough to buy food, so I took things from Alex's kitchen. I tried not to take too much because I didn't want him to notice."

"Did your mother come into the house?" Sabre asked.

"No. I kept the key because Mom wanted to drink Alex's alcohol, and I didn't want her to. The first couple of days were pretty bad." Angela grimaced, a shadow of pain in her eyes.

Sabre's heart ached for what the girl had been through, watching her mother detox. She squeezed Angela's hand. "I'm sorry, but I need to hear the rest."

"I didn't leave Mom alone even to go into the house at first because I was afraid she'd give up and run away. The second day, she finally fell asleep. I was starving, so I went to Alex's kitchen and made peanut butter and jelly sandwiches." She looked down at the floor. "I did it again the next day too and realized I'd used half a loaf of bread. I was afraid Alex would notice, but it was too late. After that, I didn't go back and get anything for a while."

The more Angela talked, the angrier Sabre got at Xander for putting her child through that. She understood addiction was an illness, but that didn't make it any less difficult on Angela. She deserved to be a kid, not a parent to her own mother.

"Why didn't you tell Alex you were here?" Sabre asked.

"We were afraid he'd turn us in."

"What was your plan? You knew you couldn't stay here forever."

"Mom said when she was ready, we could go to a shelter."

"Did she mention going to rehab?"

Angela shook her head. "She hates rehab, but she promised to go to meetings. She just needs a place to stay. Aunt Jan won't let her live at her house because she doesn't trust her."

Sabre didn't know what to say to that. She didn't blame the aunt or trust Xander either. Besides, the court wouldn't allow it. Xander would have to prove herself again, and each time she messed up, the process took longer.

"What will happen to my mom?"

"I'm not sure. She could get in trouble for running away with you."

"Will she go to jail?"

"Maybe."

"But it was my idea," Angela pleaded. "She wanted help, but it was my plan."

"I know, but you're not the adult here." The girl looked so sad and scared, Sabre quickly added, "They'll probably just try to help your mother get clean. I can't promise that, but I'll do what I can." Sabre stood. "Let's go join the others."

The kitchen counter was loaded with food. "Good timing," Griffin said. "Your sandwiches are ready."

While Angela and her mother ate, JP pulled Sabre aside and gave her a quick recap of what Xander had said. She took the blame for the escape, verifying Angela's account of what happened. She also claimed Alex knew nothing about it. They stepped back over to the counter.

"I had no idea they were here," Griffin volunteered. "I'm sure they didn't tell me because they knew I would've turned them in. Xander knows I won't tolerate her drug use or putting her child in harm's way."

Xander nodded.

"What now?" Griffin asked.

"I need to call CPS and let them know I found Angela," Sabre said. "We also need to let the police know and call Aunt Jan so she can stop worrying. Then I'll take Angela back to her house—if that's what the social worker suggests."

"And Xander?" Griffin prodded.

"We can try to find a shelter, but it's late, and they fill up quickly. First, let me call off the search."

"I'll call DuBois and let him know," JP said.

Sabre walked away, called CPS, and left a message with the answering service. Next, she called the police. As she hung up, Angela's social worker contacted her. After a brief chat, Sabre called Jan with the news.

She returned to the kitchen and put her arm around Angela. "Your aunt is waiting for you to come home."

"Am I in trouble?"

"I expect there'll be consequences, but she's not angry. She's just glad you're safe."

"I'm sure she's angry at me," Xander said. "I can't say I blame her, but I'm more worried about the police. Will they arrest me?"

"Not tonight," JP said. "Someone will contact you tomorrow. Don't run, and tell them the truth when they question you. It'll all work out."

"I will," Xander said. "I got a good start, and I plan to stay clean. I'll attend a meeting first thing in the morning."

"I called a couple of shelters that I had in my contact list," Sabre said, "but they were full. Do you have anywhere you can go tonight and not start using?"

"You can stay here," Griffin said, "in the guesthouse."

"Are you sure?" Xander asked. "I didn't treat you well the last time I saw you."

"That was my fault. I shouldn't have said what I did."

"No, I'm glad you told me."

Sabre whispered something to JP. He nodded. Sabre said, "JP will come by tomorrow morning at 9:30 and take you to a Narcotics Anonymous meeting. Will that work?"

"Yes."

Griffin gave Xander a couple of bottles of water. "I leave early in the morning, so be sure to set the alarm. And take some milk and cereal, so you can eat breakfast before you go."

Sabre walked out to the guest house with them, so they could get Angela's belongings.

~~~

JP stayed back with Griffin. "That's the second time you've blamed yourself for Xander's relapse. You're not her supplier, are you?"

"No, of course not."

"Do you want to tell me the big secret?"

"It's not mine to tell. It's Xander's."

"Does it have anything to do with Reggie?"

"No, but speaking of him, can you please not tell anyone he's the father? He wasn't involved with this, so no crime was committed."

JP thought about breaking into his house, as well as Reggie's indiscretions. "Yeah, no crime was committed," he said.

"I know a father deserves a chance to raise his children, but not the way she was conceived."
~~~

JP flashed a visual of the domination room Reggie had in his attic. "That man is lower than a snake's belly in a wagon rut."

"I couldn't have said it better myself." Griffin raised a questioning eyebrow.

"Don't worry. I won't tell. Angela doesn't need that sleaze-ball in her life."

Chapter 54

Chapter 54

Wednesday morning

JP stopped at Griffin's house, walked to the back, and knocked on Xander's door. She didn't answer. JP knocked again, afraid she'd taken off. That wouldn't have surprised him. Druggies were predictably unreliable. He was about to walk away when she opened the door.

"Sorry I took so long," Xander said "I was in the bathroom putting on makeup for the first time in weeks. I also took a long, hot shower. We were afraid to shower for fear it would run up the water bill."

JP was surprised at how good she looked. She did clean up well, as Griffin and Sabre had said.

"You look nice," JP said. They started toward his truck. "There's a meeting less than a mile from here that starts at ten, so you'll be early for that one. But if you have a particular group you want to join, we can drive there instead."

"No, it would be good to start fresh. I know too many people at some meetings. People I shouldn't be around." She paused. "I'm not blaming them. I know it's my own choice, but it'll be easier with a new group."

They got in the truck and headed out, the blue sky a good omen for Xander's fresh start. "Did you sleep okay last night?" JP asked after a few minutes of silence.

"Yes, thank you. Alex and I talked for a while. He's been very good to me."

"He seems like a good man."

JP stopped in front of a church not far away. "Here's your meeting. Do you want me to walk you in?"

"Not yet." She hesitated. "Can we talk for a minute?"

"Sure." JP checked the clock on the dash. "You have plenty of time."

"Alex told me you know about Reggie and promised not to tell. I really appreciate that. Angela doesn't need to know about my ... rape. And she doesn't need that man in her life. I'm sure he wouldn't be interested in raising her, but that doesn't mean he wouldn't make trouble for us. And I'd hate to think what he might do when she becomes a teenager."

"I agree. I'll keep your secret."

She looked around at the location. "I'm glad this is so close. I'll be able to walk here." Xander smiled for the first time. "Alex said I could stay in his guest house as long as I attend meetings and stay clean and sober. He gave me a key to the apartment, but not to the house. I can only go in there when he's home. I don't blame him. I wouldn't trust me either at this point."

"That was generous of him."

Xander sat there, still not making a move to get out.

Was she afraid to go into the meeting? "I'll attend this first one with you, if that helps."

"It's not that." She paused. "I need to tell you about Alex. He's not really my customer." Xander took a deep breath. "Yeah, he did pay me at first, but just for company. He didn't want to have sex or even kiss me. We met while I was using. He just wanted to be friends, but I wouldn't have anything to do with him unless he paid me. So, he did."

"Okay." JP waited for her to continue or stop, whichever she chose.

"After I got clean, we became real friends, and he helped me in a lot of ways. But I didn't understand why he wanted to spend time with me and Angela and not expect anything in return." Xander shook her head. "Then I slipped. I got drunk and called Alex to pick me up. He came to get me, and I was all over him, begging him to hook up with me. But he wouldn't. When I sobered up, he told me why." She stopped and was quiet for a long moment.

"You don't have to tell me," JP said. "Especially if it's something you don't want aired in court. I'm not keeping any more secrets from Sabre."

"This will all come out soon, and I'll tell the social worker when I see her today."

"Okay."

"Alex and I didn't meet accidentally." She looked over at JP. "He told you about my childhood? How I lost my parents and was raised by the Madisons?"

"Yes, he did."

"What he didn't tell you was that he lost his parents too when he was six years old. Alex was in the same accident I was in. He's my brother. He was six at the time and was raised in foster homes for several years. He bounced around a lot because he was hard to live with. He kept running away and searching for me. When he was eleven, a family took guardianship of him and kept him as their own. They convinced him to quit looking and live his own life. He did, but he never gave up on the idea and eventually found me."

"How do you know for sure you're biologically related?" JP suddenly realized they both had the same great facial features.

"When we first met, Alex bought me a drink and kept the glass. He had my DNA analyzed, and it was a match. He didn't tell me because he wasn't sure he wanted an addict for a sister. When I cleaned up, we got closer. He almost told me many times over the past few years, but he was afraid I would be ashamed of the way I used to flirt with him and not want him in my life. He wasn't willing to risk that."

"Does Angela know?"

"No, but we'll tell her soon."

"What's your plan to stay clean?"

"One day at a time."

Chapter 55

Chapter 55

Wednesday morning

"Dené, it's time to go," Sabre yelled. They were running late. JP had left earlier, taking Morgan to her school on his way to meet Xander. Now Sabre would drop off Dené at hers. The extra trip to a distant school every morning was taking a toll. When she grabbed Dené's backpack from the table, she was moving quickly and didn't notice it was open. Things came tumbling out. Two books, several pencils, and a pack of Marlboros. *What the hell?* She put everything back, except the cigarettes, which she stuck in her pocket.

Smoking? Really? The girl was only twelve, or would be soon.

Sabre was too rattled to deal with it now, and she had to get to court.

Dené wasn't the chatterbox Morgan was, and Sabre didn't really feel like making small talk. So, the ride to school was relatively quiet. When they got there, Dené thanked her and got out of the car. *One thing for sure, the girl had been taught good manners.*

~~~

Sabre finished her morning calendar and went upstairs to Voices for Children to see if Dr. Upton was around. She found him working on the computer in one of the offices.
~~~

"Hello, Sabre," the doctor said. "I'm doing more research on Eddie's case. I really hope we can come up with a diagnosis, one that can be treated."

"So, you think Eddie has been sick all this time?" Sabre asked.

"I didn't say that. I sure don't want the kid to be ill, but if he is, I want him treated. The problem is that some of his symptoms would be easy to create."

"Like what?"

"A dozen things can cause diarrhea, for instance. Or a rash. A child can be easily convinced his head hurts or his stomach aches, especially if that gets him the attention he wants from his mother."

"So, you think she may have caused some of the symptoms?"

"I didn't say that either. But I am saying it is very possible. And the pattern is such that he's sickest when he's with her. That's not a good sign."

"Did you meet with the other doctors?"

"Not yet. It was postponed until this afternoon. Something came up with the psychiatrist, and I think it's important she be there. The good news is, we've added an infectious disease specialist to the mix."

"How did you get so many doctors to help you?"

"Most are retired and bored, and none of them want to see a child suffer."

"I really appreciate your efforts. Please thank the other doctors for me as well."

"Yeah." He waved a dismissive hand.

Sabre had noticed he didn't seem to need or want accolades.

He looked up from the monitor. "I have a new disease to run past the group today."

"Care to share?"

"Not yet. There's no reason to put it out there until we have more data."

"Fair enough," Sabre said. "Just keep me posted."

~~~

After work, Sabre went straight to Dené's room to confront her about the cigarettes before Morgan got home. "Dené, we need to talk."

"What did I do now?" Dené asked defensively.

Sabre pulled the Marlboros from her pocket and held them out. "What's this?"

"Uh...cigarettes."

"I know that. Why were they in your backpack?"

She looked away. "I found them."

"Where?"

"I'd rather not say."

"Well, you need to say." Sabre raised her voice in frustration. "This is serious."

"I didn't smoke any."

"Then why keep them?"

She shrugged.

"Dené, you need to tell me where you got the cigarettes."

"She got them from my drawer," Morgan said, stepping into the room. "I'm sorry, but I was listening outside, and I can't let Dené take the blame." She turned to Dené. "Why wouldn't you tell her where you got them?"

"Because I didn't want to get you in trouble. You'll be living here a while. I may be gone soon, so no one *has* to like me."

Sabre sat on the bed next to Dené and put an arm around her shoulder. "We *all* like you, and we're learning to love you. You're an important part of this family. I know you and Morgan have had some problems, but you've had some good times too. Siblings are like that."

"But they always have each other's back, right?" Dené glanced at Morgan. "That's what I was doing. Smoking is awful."
~~~

"I know that," Morgan said.

Sabre stood and locked eyes on Morgan. "Why did you have them?"

Morgan didn't answer.

"Were you smoking?"

"No!"

"Where did you get them?"

"I don't think I should tell."

"Yes, you should," Sabre insisted. "Or you can tell Uncle Johnny."

"No, thank you." Morgan sighed. "I used the bathroom after Conner, and they were on the floor. He must've dropped them."

Sabre didn't know what to believe, but she left and went to Conner's room. "Are these yours?" She held out the pack.

"No," he said, a little indignant.

"Morgan says she found them in the bathroom after you used it. Then she hid them so you wouldn't get in trouble."

"Well, that was sweet. But it wasn't me. I don't smoke. It's gross."

"Okay, you can talk to JP when he gets home."

"Fine," Conner said. "Can I finish my homework now?"

Sabre went to the kitchen and poured herself a glass of wine. This parenting thing was frustrating. It reinforced her sense that she didn't want to bear children of her own. *How do parents do it?* The kids had all sounded so convincing, but one of them had to be lying. Sabre was used to children lying to her. It was the nature of her business. But she usually got to the truth in the end because she had evidence to confront them with. This was different. It felt personal and tugged at her heartstrings.

She had just sat down on the patio when JP came out and joined her. When she told him everything that had happened, he smiled.

"It's not funny," she said, feeling irritated.

"It kind of is. The cigarettes are mine."

"Yours?" She scoffed.

"Not exactly mine, but I'm the one who brought them into the house." He flashed another smile. "DuBois quit smoking—again. He said at ten dollars a pack, he didn't have the heart to throw them away. So, he asked me to."

Sabre smacked him lightly on his chest. "You jerk! I went through all that with the kids, and it was you. What a waste of time and energy."

"It wasn't all a waste. Didn't you say Morgan and Dené bonded over the cigarettes?"

"Actually, they bonded over the secret. Morgan was impressed that Dené covered for her. She has that kind of relationship with Conner, but I think she's forming it with Dené now too."

"See, it wasn't all bad."

"Grr... I'm still mad at you." Sabre gave him a slight smile. "I'm staying out here to drink my wine. You're making dinner."

Chapter 56

Thursday morning

When Sabre finished her last case on the morning calendar, Bob was waiting outside Department Four. "Lunch?" he asked.

"Sure."

They walked to the parking lot. "I'll drive," Bob said.

In the car, Sabre set her files down, leaned back, and tried to relax. Bob started to pull out and suddenly, she shuddered.

"What's wrong?" Bob asked.

"Stop! I'm scared."

Bob pulled back in and shut off the engine. "What's happening?"

Sabre's face felt hot, and her chest tightened.

"Do you need a doctor?"

"No, no." She took a deep breath in through her nose and let it out of her mouth in an attempt to calm herself. "I just remembered something."

"Can you tell me?"

"I heard his voice. He was saying a lot of nasty things to me and Harold." Sabre sat for a minute, trying to breathe normally. Then she picked up her files. "I need to go see JP."

"Do you want me to drive you?"

"No." She pulled in a short, deep breath and blew it out. "I'm okay. Sorry."

"Do you have court this afternoon?"

"No. I'll see you tomorrow."

"I'll check later to make sure you're okay."

Sabre called JP on the way to her car. "I experienced another memory and need to see you."

"I'm at a coffee shop with DuBois, not far from juvenile court," he said. "Why don't you meet us here?"

"Okay."

Sabre got the directions and left. On her drive, she took deep breaths, saying "calm, relax" and "in control," just as the hypnotherapist had taught her. By the time she reached the coffee shop, much of her fear had subsided.

JP met her at the door, gave her a hug, and led her to where DuBois was sitting. Sabre greeted him and sat down. A cup of hot tea was already on the table.

"I ordered you chamomile with lavender. The barista said it was the best for stress."

"This is just what I needed," she said. "Thank you."

After a few moments, Sabre explained what she had remembered. "I still didn't see his face because of the mask, and for whatever other reason, he's blurry. I remember his words, but not really his voice, except that it has a familiar ring. I know this sounds crazy, because I can't really hear the voice, but somehow I feel like I should recognize it." She took a moment to sip her tea. "The message though is clear—a lot of foul language and racial slurs against Harold. And the guy kept calling me a *bitch*. He seemed hung up on women's body parts, because I heard that a lot too."

"The physical description you gave us is pretty general, but it fits Porter and Gunner Holloway, as well as Lynch," JP said. "We thought we eliminated Gunner with his alibi, but he could've prompted people at the bar to lie for him."

"The description fits a million other men," DuBois added. "We do cut that population down with the left-handed or ambidextrous thing."

"That still puts Gunner in the running because he's left-handed," JP said. "I asked Lynch's neighbor to check which hand the guy uses. He's pretty certain Lynch is left-handed but will verify it. As for Porter, I've only seen him use his right hand."

"I forgot to tell you," DuBois said. "I spoke to Mrs. Holloway. She said Porter's fully ambidextrous. He played his baseball career mostly throwing with his left hand. He batted both ways."

"So, they're all still possibilities," JP said.

"What about the blue Ford truck?" DuBois asked.

Sabre shook her head. "I don't know vehicles enough to say for sure. I know a few emblems, but I don't recall seeing one. And the truck wasn't in the canyon. When I get the flash of the truck, it's on the street near Angela's house. It may not even be related."

"True," JP said, "but it scared you."

"Maybe that's just because it gave me the feeling it was following me."

"So, the man may or may not have a blue truck." DuBois shook his head. "I ran his description through the database of violent offenders, but it's too large a group to work with."

Sabre took another drink of tea and tried to conjure up more memories, but it never seemed to work when she tried. They just came to her at the strangest times.

JP sat staring at his coffee cup.

"Hello," DuBois said.

Sabre and JP both looked up.

"What?" JP asked.

"You both seemed to drift off."

"I'm sorry," Sabre said. "If we're done here, I'm going home. I have a big case on calendar tomorrow that needs my attention."

"And I have a hunch to follow up on." JP stood.

"Something I should know about?" DuBois asked.

"Not yet. If I get anything, you'll be the first to know."

Chapter 57

Chapter 57

Thursday afternoon

In his truck, JP called Ron. "I need you for more surveillance on Reggie."

"But you found Angela. Do you still think he might be involved?"

"If he knows he's the father, he might have gone after Sabre. And he fits the general description from Sabre's memory."

"You think he could've killed Harold?"

"Maybe. It seems too coincidental that the attack took place near Angela's house. The perp might've just been following her and grabbed her before she went inside, but it's also possible he wanted to stop her from going in."

"What would he gain from that?"

"Maybe he wanted to confirm that he was the father. He might've thought Sabre knew."

"What do you want me to do?"

"Just follow Reggie and see if he does anything unusual."

"Unusual? Really?"

"Right. The man's a creep."

"I'm on it, boss."

~~~

Thursday evening
~~~

After an early dinner of takeout pizza, the girls ran to their room to get ready to go out. They had talked Conner into taking them to a new Disney movie.

"Drive safe, Conner," Sabre said. "And come right home after the movie. It's a school night."

A few minutes later, the house was blissfully quiet. "I guess it's just the two of us for a change," JP said.

"It's kind of nice. What would you like to do?"

"You probably won't like it."

"What?"

"Karaoke night at the Hay Bale." He grinned.

"Let's go."

"You really want to go along?" JP seemed surprised.

"Isn't that the bar where Porter Holloway hangs out?"

"Yep."

"He's the most likely suspect we have, right?"

"One of a couple."

"And he doesn't know me," Sabre said.

"Uh… unless he does."

"Oh right." Sabre had second thoughts. "If he is the perp, he does know me."

"Maybe I should go alone."

Sabre shook her head, refusing to be intimidated. "Let's go together. We'll stay back and watch him when he takes the stage. Maybe it'll trigger something for me." She paused. "Or we could let him see me and check how he reacts."

"No!" JP jumped up. "That'll only make him think we're on to him, and who knows what he'll do. So far, the perp hasn't made other attempts to go after you."

"Which means he's probably a stranger."

"Or someone who knows you've lost your memory."

"That's a short list."

"When we get back, I'll start working on it. Or we can bag this idea, stay home, and work on it now."

"I'm going," Sabre said, grabbing her jacket. "You coming with me?"

"Okay, but we're not getting close to him."

Chapter 58

Thursday night

When Sabre and JP walked into the bar, a woman was doing a sloppy version of Carrie Underwood's *Jesus Take the Wheel*. JP glanced around.

"Do you see him?" Sabre asked.

"Not yet, but apparently, he doesn't miss many karaoke nights—his chance to be in the spotlight."

"Then we should move away from the door in case he walks in."

"There he is," JP said, nodding toward the end of the counter.

"I don't see him."

"Because you're too short. Let's grab that table." JP moved toward the stage. "It'll be perfect. He's not likely to pass by, and I'll still be able to keep him in my sights."

They were only seated a few minutes when a waitress approached to take their order. Sabre asked for water. When JP ordered a beer, she studied his face, then gave him a knowing glance, and said, "Oh yeah, you're that guy."

JP just nodded.

"What was that about?" Sabre asked when she left.

"She's the waitress Porter was harassing the night DuBois and I were here."

"Right," Sabre said jokingly. "You're *that* guy." She smiled. She trusted JP more than she'd ever trusted any man. That was a good thing, because women always flirted with him. She stared for a moment, admiring his face.

"What?"

"You're so handsome, movie-star handsome."

"Stop it."

Even in the poor lighting, she could tell he'd blushed. He was confident about most things and knew his own strengths, but he really had no idea just how good-looking he was.

The waitress returned shortly, apparently making their table her first stop. She delivered a beer, a bottle of Perrier mineral water, and a chilled glass with ice.

The waitress spoke directly to Sabre. "I took the liberty of getting you Perrier." She turned to face JP. "Thank you for standing up to Porter. This round is on me."

JP tried to tip her, but she refused. She started to walk away just as Porter's name was called to sing. "And there he is," she said sarcastically.

Sabre watched intently as Porter stepped up on the small platform. He wore a black t-shirt with the sleeves cut off, exposing his tattoos.

"What's that on his left arm?" Sabre asked.

"It looks like a torn version of a Confederate flag."

"It's red." Sabre swallowed. She sat silently, staring at Porter.

"Are you okay?" JP asked.

"I'm fine."

"Does he look familiar?"

"He looks like his father."

"Anything else? No memories?"

She shook her head. "I was prepared to feel something. To remember something. But I got nothing. I'm not saying it wasn't him, because he fits the description, especially the red on his upper arm. But there are lots of red tattoos—roses, snakes, American flags."

JP pushed his chair back. "I can't take much more of his caterwaulin'."

"I'm ready." Sabre stood. She started toward the exit, then glanced back to see JP put money under his half-empty beer bottle. She smiled, knowing he would leave a tip. It wasn't in his nature not to.

~~~

Reggie had left work an hour after Ron started watching for him at the warehouse. Ron had followed, expecting him to go home, but instead Reggie drove downtown and turned into the same parking garage as before. Ron pulled in too and parked ten spaces away. He stayed in his car for a few minutes, then tailed Reggie a few blocks to the Star Bar, careful to stay out of sight. Reggie might find it strange to see him near the same bar at the same time again. Once inside, Ron wouldn't be as concerned. Most people frequented familiar drinking holes, trying to get that *Cheers*-like feeling.

Reggie got a beer at the counter and sat alone for ten minutes. He had apparently ordered food as well, because a waitress soon brought him a plate, along with another beer. Ron watched more closely this time, observing that he held his fork in his left hand when he ate. When Reggie finished his food, he started to mingle. The bar had started to fill with Happy Hour customers, making the pickings better for a man on the prowl, which is how Ron perceived him.

Reggie moved around, talking to people he knew and some who appeared to be strangers to him. Once he came so close, Ron had to turn his back. Reggie hit on a few girls, then moved on when they showed no interest.

A little after eight, he gave up and left the bar. Again, Ron stayed back. He knew where Reggie's car was parked, so Ron took a slightly different route to reach the parking garage.

After Reggie left the parking garage, Ron lost him for a while, then spotted the Mustang, going in the direction of the freeway, not the Werewolf. Reggie sped out of his sight
~~~

a couple of times, but soon Ron was confident his subject was headed home. When he turned onto his own street, Ron dropped back, pulled over, and waited. Two minutes later, he parked across from Reggie's house just as the garage door started to close. And there he sat for the next hour and a half.

Finally, JP called. "Where are you?"

"I'm across the street from Reggie's house. Nothing eventful happened at the bar, except that he ate his food with his left hand."

"That's something," JP said. "It's nearly ten o'clock. He's probably done for the night. You can go home."

"That works for me," Ron said.

"Are you busy tomorrow night?"

"I might have plans, but I could probably change them if you need me."

"I'll check with you tomorrow. If you can't do it, maybe I'll do the surveillance myself. Then, if necessary, maybe you can watch him on Saturday."

"What do you expect to see?" Ron asked.

"I don't know. I hate to think what he does to those poor young girls he brings home with him. As far as this case is concerned, I'm grasping at straws, but I'm not ready to give up on this guy. Maybe it's because he's such a creep."

Chapter 59

Chapter 59

Friday morning

Sabre approached Bob as soon as he arrived at juvenile court. She handed him the social study. "Take a quick look at this. Dr. Upton wants to talk to both of us before the hearing."

"Where is he?" Bob asked.

"Upstairs in the CASA office. We can use a private room there."

They climbed the steps together, Bob trying to read as he walked. He stopped at the top and studied the paperwork.

"Does this mean what I think it does?" Bob flipped to the end to see the recommendations. "Wait. The recs haven't changed."

"Let's hear what the doctor has to say, then we can decide what to do."

Dr. Upton got right down to business, as always. "Eddie has all the symptoms of Mast Cell Activation Syndrome. A lot of these symptoms are also common to many allergies, the itching skin and rash, watery, irritated eyes, runny nose, swelling in his throat, and trouble breathing. There are times when he would have severe headaches and show signs of confusion or have cramps, nausea, and diarrhea. Many of the symptoms which are more common with MCAS were reported by the mother. Sometimes they were present when the doctor saw the child, sometimes they were not. And the treatment seems to be more effective when his mother is not present."

That was odd. "Has he been tested for it?" Sabre asked.

"There are no definitive tests, but Eddie meets all the requirements for an MCAS diagnosis. We look for three different things, all of which Eddie has." The doctor used his fingers to stress his points. "He has allergy symptoms in two or more organ systems that keep coming back. He has higher than normal levels of tryptase and histamines. He gets better after using antihistamine medications that block chemicals released by mast cells."

"What causes it?" Sabre asked.

"The exact cause is unknown. It's an idiopathic disease, and there's not enough information to know if it is genetic. It's difficult to pinpoint the exact thing that triggers the allergic reactions, and new ones come up all the time." Dr. Upton took a breath. "Mast cells are immune cells, and their primary role is to trigger inflammatory responses to defend the body against pathogens and allergens. When foreign bodies are present, mast cells respond by releasing mediators. In people with MCAS, the immune system inappropriately activates mast cells, releasing too many mediators, causing severe allergic reactions."

Bob spoke up. "What kind of treatment does Eddie need?"

"It's more about diet and lifestyle than medication. He needs to avoid foods high in histamines, such as leftovers, cured meats, and canned fish. The allergist will provide Eddie's caretaker with a complete list. Besides that, he needs to avoid extreme temperatures, molds, medications with high histamine levels, and common preservatives. Fresh food is the best choice, but he still has to be careful of shellfish, nuts, citrus, and other high-histamine foods."

"Wow," Sabre said. "That's a lot."

"Yes, but with close attention, his caretaker can determine what affects him, with the proviso, of course, that new things can come up every day."

"You keep saying *caretaker*," Sabre said. "Do you think the mother can provide the care Eddie needs?"

"She would likely pay the closest attention to his needs. However, one of the problems may be that, in a sense, Eddie is allergic to his mother."

"What?" Bob looked stunned. "Is that possible?"

"It is, on very rare occasions. Most likely, he is allergic to her saliva. I observed the mother and son together on two different occasions, and both times, they shared food or drink. They would have to stop that behavior and see if things got better. If we determine that he is allergic to her, rather than just her saliva, then distance would be the only effective remedy." Dr. Upton looked skeptical. "I'm not fully on board with human-to-human allergies, but there is some evidence that it's possible."

"If that's the case, why was Eddie better when they were in the desert for that week? You would think if he was only around his mother in that small space, he would've been worse."

"Like I said, it's more likely her saliva or what's in her saliva. It's possible that if she eats or drinks something that Eddie is allergic to, then he consumes the same item after she's contaminated it, that he could have an allergic reaction. It's very possible they didn't have anything with them that he was allergic to. I'm sure they had limited supplies. Or, maybe he didn't eat or drink after her that week."

Sabre took a moment to process all that.

"My client is willing to do whatever is necessary to help her son," Bob said.

"She seems very cooperative," Upton commented. "She's also very angry at the medical system, and with good reason. Hopefully, we can provide the medical treatment Eddie needs now."

"Can he be cured?" Sabre asked.

"Unfortunately not, and the disease will likely get worse with time. All we can do is treat him with certain medications. And we have to be careful with those because they often work for a while, then stop being effective and possibly make things worse."

"What are your recommendations?" Bob asked. "Are they different from the social worker's?"

"I read the report, and she didn't have all the information we have now when she wrote it, but as far as I know, she hasn't given any new recommendations. Mine would vary considerably from hers, but I still need more time."

"Tell me this," Bob said. "Is it your opinion that the mother hasn't done anything intentional or neglectful to hurt this child?"

"I don't see anything that indicates she has Factitious Disorder, if that's what you're asking. But we need more time to determine if the mother is a danger to her child because of a possible human-to-human allergy."

"Can you test for that?" Sabre asked.

"Yes, in a controlled environment."

"In the meantime, what do you recommend?" Sabre asked.

"I'm new to the process, but it's my opinion that we leave Eddie right where he is until we test the mother."

"How long will that take?" Bob asked.

"A few days, but including setup time, maybe a few weeks."

"If Eddie is allergic to her, then what?"

"We have to come up with a solution where the mother and her child can have time together in a controlled space."

"What if Eddie is not allergic to his mother, but only to her saliva?" Sabre asked. "Then what would you recommend?"

"I believe the mother is the best person to provide for his well-being. She is the only one who will be dedicated enough to watch him closely and make the sacrifices that will be needed for this child."

"Have you told that to the social worker?" Sabre asked.

"Yes, but she doesn't agree with me. She thinks the court should go forward with jurisdiction. She said it's a placement issue."

"What?" Bob bristled. "I'll talk to that little twerp. It's the *whole* jurisdictional issue."

"That's what I thought," Dr. Upton said. "But it's not my area of expertise, so I didn't argue with her."

"She's young and new and doesn't want to relinquish any power to you," Bob said. "She wants to call the shots." He stood and started for the door. "I have to go straighten her out."

"Bob, let it be," Sabre said. "Ultimately, Dave Casey will give her a reality check. Let's go to court."

~~~

Once the Eddie Blane case was called, Sabre explained the new development, then requested a continuance based on the information provided by the CASA worker. "Dr. Upton is in court, Your Honor, if you have any questions."

"Thank you," Judge Hekman said. "Dr. Upton, do you have anything to add to what minor's counsel has said?"

"Only that I have kept Eddie's primary doctor in the loop, and he appears to be in full agreement with my team's assessment."

"Does anyone object to a continuance?" the judge asked.

"On behalf of the mother, I join minor's counsel in the request," Bob said.

Dave Casey stood. "The Department would like to go forward today. Perhaps the mother's attorney wants to set a trial date for jurisdiction."

Judge Hekman frowned at him, never one to hold back.

"I'll set it for trial if that's what the court wants, Your Honor," Bob said. "But today, I'm asking for a continuance. I
~~~

think once all the reports are in, there will be no need for a trial."

Judge Hekman addressed Dr. Upton. "How long do you need to finish your tests?"

"Two weeks should be plenty of time. We've already completed part of them."

"The case is continued for two weeks from today," the judge ordered. "This court is adjourned."

Chapter 60

Chapter 60

Friday night

JP called Ron and asked, "Can you do a surveillance tonight?"

"I made plans, but I can change them if you really need me."

"What kind of plans?"

"I'm going out with a friend and his wife. I think they're trying to set me up with someone they know. I'm not sure I even want to go, but they assured me it wouldn't be anything uncomfortable, just a group thing."

"You may meet the love of your life," JP said.

"Fat chance."

"One thing's for certain, you won't meet anyone on a stakeout."

"Reggie again?" Ron asked.

"You're right as rain."

"Do you really think he may have been the one who attacked Sabre?"

"If he has figured out he's Angela's father, then it's a possibility."

"But not likely," Ron said. "What's his motive?"

"Maybe he just thinks he might be the father, and wanted to know for sure."

"Do you think he wants his kid?"

"Some men just want the ownership of their children. Or, more likely, he wants a way to have Xander in his life."

"That's possible, but I think you just don't trust the guy because of what you found in the attic. Do you?"

"Not as far as I can throw him. But I have to find out what happened to Sabre, and he's the only lead I can act on." JP decided Ron should go on his date. "It's not that important. Don't change your plans. I'll surveil him for a while, and if need be, you can take a shift another night."

~~~

JP kept an eye on Reggie in the crowded Star Bar. Reggie wandered around for fifteen minutes, then zeroed in on a woman who looked far too young to be in the bar. Reggie bought her a couple of drinks. JP watched closely, but never saw him spike her glass. He apparently didn't need to. She was getting tipsy without it.

A little before midnight, Reggie left with the girl. JP followed. Since he hadn't tailed Reggie to the bar, he didn't know where he'd parked. JP stayed behind him until the couple reached his Mustang and got in. JP dashed back to his truck, which was a block and a half away. Instead of trying to follow, he drove directly toward Reggie's house. If the punk was there, he wasn't sure what he would do. If not, he would just go home.

When JP reached Reggie's place, he and the young woman were just getting out of the car. Shortly after, the garage door closed behind them.

JP waited and watched, wondering if he should leave, but he had a bad feeling, probably because he knew the guy was a scumbag who hurt women. It could be happening every night. Why would tonight be any different? He waited and watched. There was not much movement except for a few shadows in the front room at first.

JP wanted to break into the house and pummel Reggie. *What if he forced her into his den of iniquity?*
~~~

An hour later, JP was chomping at the bit. He was about to get out of the car when the half-clothed girl ran out of the house, clutching her chest, holding her sweater closed. JP started his truck, and a moment later, Reggie bolted out. It was all he could do to keep from ramming into the scumbag.

"Hey, wait!" Reggie called.

The girl kept running, and Reggie sprinted after her. JP pulled his truck up next to her. "Do you need help?"

She jumped into his truck. "Go!" she shouted.

JP sped off, leaving Reggie behind in the street.

"He raped me," she said, tears rolling down her cheeks. "I k... kept telling him no, but he wouldn't stop."

JP didn't know whether to question her or just let her talk. As a detective, he'd want the information as soon as possible. He wished Sabre were there. She was good with young victims. "Look, if you need to talk, I'm here to listen, but don't feel pressured to tell me the details if you'd rather not," JP said. "Either way, I'm taking you to the hospital to get checked out or to the police station, so you can report him."

"I don't know if I want to do that."

"I know this guy. I was watching his house on an unrelated case, but I have reason to believe he's raped other girls. You just confirmed that. He needs to be stopped."

"Are you a cop?"

"I used to be. Now I'm a private investigator. I just happened to be here."

"Can't you just take me to my car?" She sobbed. "Wh... What if the cops don't believe me? I've been drinking, and I'm underage."

"All the more reason I shouldn't drop you off. You can't drive in the state you're in. The police will believe you. Trust me. You can't let him get away with this. He'll just keep doing it to others."

She took a deep breath and whimpered, "Okay. Take me to the police station." Light from a streetlamp streamed across her face. For the first time, JP got a good look at her. She had a swollen eye and a bloody lip and looked even younger than he'd thought earlier.

"He hit you?"

"Several times. Every time I said no, he hit me again. I finally stopped saying anything. I just kept trying to get away."

She cried for a minute, then sat in silence. JP finally introduced himself, and she told him her name was Kirsten Norris.

"How old are you?"

"I just turned seventeen, but I have a fake ID."

"Do you want to call your parents and have them meet you at the station?"

"No," she said softly.

"Is there anyone you can call to come be with you?"

She shook her head.

When they reached the police station, Kirsten just sat there.

"You'll be okay," JP said. "This part will be hard, but you'll get through it."

"Will you go in with me?" she asked.

"Of course." He'd planned to go in and make sure she got the help she needed, but he was glad she'd asked.

Chapter 61

Saturday afternoon

Sabre and JP parked at the police station to see Detective DuBois. Sabre had remembered seeing the license plate on the blue truck. She could only recall the first three letters, but that would narrow it down. DuBois had something he wanted to talk to JP about as well.

They were about to go inside the building when Sabre spotted Jan Webb. *What was Angela's aunt doing here?* She was speaking to a blond man. They turned and started to walk.

"Oh my God." Sabre shook with fear. "That's him."

"Who?" JP asked.

"The man in the canyon. The guy who killed Harold! That's him with Jan." Sabre kept repeating the words. Her shoulders sagged, and she felt weak. She reached for JP, but he pulled away.

"I remember everything," Sabre said.

JP was already out of the truck.

"Reggie!" he yelled.

The blond man stopped and turned around. "What?"

JP rushed forward, grabbed him, and pinned him against the wall.

"What the hell?" Reggie said.

Sabre steeled her nerves and got out of the truck. She didn't want to see the killer up close, but she couldn't stop herself. Two uniformed cops ran toward them, as Jan yelled at JP to leave the guy alone. Reggie screamed profanities, triggering Sabre's fear again. But in all the chaos, she didn't understand why Jan was there.

"What's going on?" An officer asked.

Reggie kept yelling at JP to let him go.

"Calm down!" the officer demanded.

"I'm a retired cop," JP said. "My ID is in my wallet in my back pocket. Feel free to look. This man is a suspect in a murder investigation that Detective DuBois is handling."

"What are you talking about?" Jan said. "He's not a suspect in a murder case."

"I'm afraid he is," JP said. "Officer, please contact DuBois. He's expecting me."

"You can't just hold him there," Jan said. "Let him go."

The female cop said, "I'll get DuBois."

The male officer stepped close to Reggie. "If he lets go, you gonna run? Because I really don't feel like a chase today."

"I'm not letting him go until DuBois gets here," JP said.

"He didn't kill anyone," Jan whined. "He just got out on bail for trumped up rape charges."

"Shut up, Jan!" Reggie shouted. "I don't need your help."

"Rape?" The cop tensed.

"Yep," JP said. "He was arrested last night."

"Get on the ground!" The cop grabbed Reggie. "We'll let DuBois sort this out."

Sabre sat down on a nearby half-wall. Her head was spinning with memories.

Jan walked over. "Do you know what's going on?"

"I do," Sabre said. "But what I don't understand is why you're with that man."

"He's my boyfriend. His name's Reggie Younger."

"How long have you known him?"

"Most of my life. He worked with my father when I was young. I had a crush on him back then, but he was older than me and not interested. We got reacquainted about six months ago."

"Do you know him well? I mean, have you seen a lot of him?"

"We go out once a week. I'd like more, but he's busy with work and taking care of his elderly parents. I don't understand why JP is accusing him of murder. He's not like that. Why would JP do that?"

"Because Reggie killed a man—and I saw him do it."

"No!" Jan gasped and clutched her sweater. "What about the rape?"

"He did that too. JP was watching his house and helped the girl when she escaped. I didn't know until now he was the man who killed Harold."

Detective DuBois hurried around the corner with the female cop. Sabre stood and walked with them.

"Who is this guy?" DuBois asked.

"Reggie Younger. I recognized him as the man who killed Harold. And there's more. I remember everything."

"There's no doubt in your mind?"

"None."

DuBois reached the scene. Reggie was face down on the ground, and the officer had a foot on his back. "Thanks," DuBois said. "I'll take him from here." He slapped handcuffs on Reggie and jerked him to his feet. "You're under arrest for murder."

Chapter 62

Chapter 62

Saturday afternoon

"Reggie's in a holding cell," DuBois said. "He can wait there until we're done. I need to hear everything you remember."

They were in a small conference room in the police station. Someone had brought Sabre a bottle of water, but she hadn't opened it yet. She was still reeling. She took a deep breath and recalled that day. "I left my office and drove to see Angela. I was distracted because I thought I might be pregnant."

"What?" JP asked, mouth open.

"Don't worry, I'm not. But I wasn't as alert as usual because I was anxious to get home and take a test. There wasn't a space in front of Angela's house, so I parked on a side street behind a blue Ford truck. I sat there for a second, thinking about everything I had to do, and staring at the license plate. That must be why the number stuck in my brain."

"It's the one you gave me?" DuBois asked.

"Yes."

"Okay, go on."

"I got out and started to walk to Angela's, but I forgot I had a gift for her, so I turned back. When I opened the passenger door, I felt a hard piece of metal against my back. I froze and waited for him to say something. The smell of woodsy cologne and body odor made me think it was a man."

"What did he say?" DuBois asked.

"He whispered, 'I have a gun. Do exactly what I say or I'll kill you, then I'll kill Angela, the little girl in the window.'"

"He called her by name?"

"Yes." Sabre realized for the first time that Reggie had targeted her.

"Then what?"

"He told me to walk around the car and get in the driver's seat. He repeated that he would kill me and Angela if I ran or did anything to draw attention. So, I walked around the car. I thought about ducking down and screaming, but I didn't know if Angela was still in the window. I was afraid he would shoot her, so I did what he said. My main thought was to get away from the area so he couldn't hurt Angela. That way, only one of us would die." She swallowed. "Then I saw Harold about fifty feet away. He was watching us, but I didn't know how much he saw. I mouthed *Help Me*, and he tilted his head, as if trying to understand. I did it again, but by then I had rounded the car and couldn't look directly at him."

"Did you see Harold after that?" DuBois asked. "I mean, before you got to the canyon."

"No."

"The neighbor, the one Angela calls Fishing Boy, saw Harold suddenly take off running down the street," JP said.

"Maybe he saw the gun or was able to tell you were in distress," DuBois said.

She paused. "I got Harold killed, didn't I?"

"No," JP said adamantly.

DuBois joined in his protest. "Harold's death is not your fault. He did what he felt he had to do. Think about the many times you've protected children. Good human beings just do the right thing when someone is in danger."

Sabre took a drink of water before she went on. "Once we were in the car, he kept the gun pointed at me."

"Did you see his face then?"

"He was still wearing the medical mask, but I saw his eyes, Reggie's eyes." She shuddered. "I asked him where we were going, but he just said 'you'll see.' He told me to drive out of the complex and turn left. I asked him how he knew Angela, and he shouted that I already knew that. I didn't know what he meant. I still don't."

JP and DuBois exchanged glances.

"But you two know, don't you?" Sabre stared at JP. "That's why you've been watching Reggie."

"He's Angela's father," JP said. "I'll explain the rest when you're done."

The man had threatened to kill his own daughter? Sabre shuddered.

"Did you drive directly to the canyon?" Dubois prompted.

"Yes. That's when I realized he would likely kill me. I tried to turn into the parking lot at the base, but he backhanded me with the gun and grabbed the wheel with the other. He managed to maneuver the car enough to keep it heading into the canyon. I tried to crash, but he kept hitting me on the head and the shoulder and shouting obscenities. I kept fighting for control and finally drove the car toward the trees. He kept us from crashing head on by smashing my leg with the butt of the gun and knocking my foot off the accelerator. When the car stopped, he hit me again."

Sabre's mouth felt dry, and she gulped more water.

"Take your time," DuBois said.

"I think I passed out for a few seconds because the next thing I knew, Reggie was dragging me out of the car." She stopped.

"Are you okay?" JP gently squeezed her hand.

"Do you need a break?" DuBois asked. "We're in no hurry. That scumbag can wait all day as far as I'm concerned."

Sabre shook her head, then took a deep breath in through her nose and exhaled through her mouth, mentally reciting her mantras. *Calm. Relax. In control.*

"Let's get this over with." She plunged back in. "Reggie pushed me against the car and pointed the gun right at my face. He unzipped his pants, pulled his penis out, and demanded that I suck him. I told him I would bite it off, and he backhanded me again across the face. That time he hit my nose, and the blood started gushing. That's when he pinned me against the car, keeping the gun pressed against my throat. He pushed so hard, the door handle hurt my back. Then he reached under my skirt and yanked down my panties. The whole time, he... he talked, telling me what he would do. He was very graphic, even exaggerating the size of his dick."

Sabre felt JP tense with anger, then fidget in his seat. She knew he wished he'd killed the guy when he'd had a chance. The only way she could tell the story was to unfold it step by step, but she knew she had to finish before he exploded.

"He didn't rape me," she blurted. "Harold suddenly appeared behind him and hit Reggie on the head with a rock. Reggie staggered and fell, and I glanced around for his gun. But it was starting to get dark, and I didn't see it. Harold yelled for me to run, but I hesitated. I didn't want to leave him behind after he'd just saved me. Then Reggie grabbed Harold's leg, pulled him to the ground, and started pounding on him. He was so enraged. I tried to get him to stop, but he kicked me, and I flew back into the bushes. I scrambled to my feet, but not before Reggie got up and came after me like a madman. He grabbed me and started smacking me around, describing how he would make me suffer for what I'd done."

Another deep breath.

"You're doing great," DuBois said.

JP fumed silently.

"Reggie slammed me against a tree and was tearing at my clothes when Harold jumped on his back. They were flailing around, and the whole time Harold was yelling at me to run, but I couldn't get myself to leave him behind." She paused and fought back tears. "I messed up, didn't I?"

"You mean that's not what happened?" DuBois asked.

"I mean, I should've done something different. Reggie didn't have the gun then. I should've looked for it and turned it on him. Maybe Harold would still be alive."

"Or maybe you'd both be dead," JP said.

"Please go on, if you can." DuBois' tone was gentle.

"Reggie and Harold were punching each other. Harold was quick, but Reggie was bigger and dominated him. I know I was a distraction to Harold because every time he saw me, he would yell at me to run, and then he'd take another hard punch." Sabre sighed. "Reggie must have spotted his gun because he leaped toward the tree where he'd dropped it and grabbed it by the barrel. Harold flew at him, and Reggie smacked his shoulder with the gun. While Harold struggled to keep his balance, Reggie flipped the gun around and pointed it at him, threatening to kill him. I jumped on Reggie from behind, but he flung me off."

Sabre took a drink of water.

"You okay?" JP asked.

Sabre nodded and went on. "Harold continued to yell at me to run. Finally, I just took off. I thought about going to Angela's to get help, but I didn't want to put her in danger. So, I kept going down the hill toward the shopping center. It was difficult running in my pumps, so I stopped and took my shoes off. That was when I heard a gunshot."

Harold's face kept flashing across her mind. *If Only...* Sabre took a deep breath. "By the time I got to the shopping center, I realized I had dropped a shoe. I kept watching for someone chasing me, and every car that came from that direction forced me into the bushes or behind buildings. I was confused and scared and in shock. And you know the rest."

Chapter 63

Chapter 63

Sunday morning

"What do you have on your agenda this morning?" Sabre asked as JP got out of bed.

"I thought I'd go to the shooting range and pretend the target is Reggie Younger."

"That's healthy, I think," Sabre said.

"By the way, DuBois said they found your missing files when they searched Reggie's house."

"All three of them? Because I remember putting them in my trunk before I left."

"Yes. They were all there. I'm not sure why he would take them, but who knows? He's a sick man. I'll pick them up for you tomorrow."

"I'd appreciate that." Sabre stood. "Would you mind hanging out with the girls for a while? Conner has plans, and I'd like to check on Angela and talk to Jan."

"That's fine."

Sabre got dressed, grabbed a piece of toast, and headed out. It felt strange driving back to Angela's house. It was the first time she'd been there since her memory returned. She suddenly relived it all again. She could see Harold standing by the rock. Sabre choked back tears, got her composure, and walked to the door.

Jan invited her in, apologizing over and over.

"It's okay. I'd like to see Angela first, then talk to you, if you don't mind."

"That's fine." Jan led Sabre upstairs to Angela's room and then left.

"What? No costume today?"

"I haven't decided yet. I'm thinking about being a southern belle." The girl took out a yellow, billowy dress and a wide-brimmed hat. "What do you think?"

"Beautiful."

"Or maybe a mermaid." Angela pulled a shiny, green formal out of her closet. The dress was tied off at the bottom to make it look like a tail.

Angela sure was creative. "Where do you get all this?"

"The thrift store. I went there yesterday with Nevaeh and her mom. Aunt Jan gave me ten dollars, and I got a lot of cool stuff."

"You sure did."

"Is Aunt Jan okay?" Angela asked. "She seemed pretty upset when she picked me up yesterday, and again this morning."

"She'll be okay. It's grownup stuff. You don't need to worry."

That seemed to appease Angela, because she changed the subject. "My mom is in rehab, you know. I get to talk to her every night. Only for a few minutes, but it's good."

"You seem pretty pleased that she's in rehab."

"She always gets better when she goes. That means we'll be able to live together again soon."

"I'm sure you're looking forward to that." Sabre was careful not to make any promises, because she knew how often parents failed.

"I like it here with Aunt Jan, but I'd rather be with my mother. And Uncle Alex is going to help us this time."

"That's good." Sabre stood to go. "I think I'd go with the mermaid." She went downstairs and joined Jan in the living room.

"I'm so sorry about Reggie," Jan said. "I had no idea. He always seemed nice, a little egotistical, but sweet to me. I realize now he was only using me."

"Stop beating yourself up. Reggie has been perfecting his act for years."

"Still, I'm old enough to know better. When he didn't try to sleep with me, I should've realized something was wrong. I just thought he was being a gentleman. What a fool I am."

"The important thing is that it's over now, and Angela is safe."

"Can she still stay here?" Jan asked. "I know I messed up big time, but it would be hard on Angela to end up in foster care."

"I've spoken to the social worker, and we don't see a need for a change. Xander is already in a rehab center, and she'll be there at least thirty days. When they release her, she can live with Alex in his guest house. When Xander's ready, Angela will be able to move in with her."

"I talked to my sister on the phone, and she seems determined to get it right this time. She asked me not to say anything to Angela about Reggie. I assured her I would never do that. It isn't my place."

"Mine either," Sabre said. "If Xander decides to tell her someday, that'll be between them. I expect Reggie will be put away for a lot of years, maybe even life."

Chapter 64

Chapter 64

Six days later

After the family finished breakfast together, Conner left to go somewhere with friends. Dené and Morgan were waiting for Travis to pick them up. Morgan was still in their room, and Dené was waiting in the living area.

"Are you ready?" Sabre asked.

"Yes. Travis should be here any minute."

Morgan walked in with her head hanging. She was holding something behind her back.

"What is it?" Sabre asked.

"I need to apologize to Dené."

"For what?"

Morgan displayed a pink journal and handed it to Dené. "I'm sorry," Morgan said. "I just found this by the side of my bed. I should never have accused you of taking it. Can you forgive me?"

"Sure," Dené said. The doorbell rang. "Let's go. Travis is here."

Morgan smiled, waved goodbye, and zipped out the door.

"I'm glad that's settled," Sabre said. "I'm off to see Velma." She gave JP a quick kiss and left.

~~~

When everyone was gone, JP took the dog outside to romp around a bit. A few minutes later, his phone rang.
~~~

"Are you busy?" DuBois asked.

"Just piddling around the house."

"Good, you can help me."

"Do what?"

"I told a friend I'd help her move. Mostly load a truck and trailer."

Of all the things people asked of him, he really hated moving people. They always seemed so indecisive. "Sure, what the heck?" JP said.

"I'll be right there to pick you up."

JP worked in his garage while he waited for DuBois and suddenly wished he'd turned down the moving gig. But it was too late now, and he knew DuBois would do the same for him if he asked.

About fifteen minutes later, DuBois showed up, and they drove off together, going east.

"Who's the friend?" JP asked.

"Just a friend," DuBois said, then changed the subject. "Did I tell you that Reggie is being charged with murder, attempted rape, assault and battery, and five counts of rape?"

"Five?"

"When Holly found out about Kirsten, it gave her the courage to report what happened to her. Two other girls from his current place of employment, plus one from the last job, accused him, too. Those cases will be harder than Kirsten's because no rape kits were done on two of them. There was one thing they all agreed upon."

"That he talked the whole time?" JP asked.

"Exactly. What an idiot. I don't know if that's his calling card, or if he had to talk to keep himself pumped up."

"I'm just glad it wasn't worse for Sabre. I'll always be grateful to Harold. It's a shame he had to die. Sabre and I offered to pay his funeral expenses, but his friend, Velma, said she had plenty of money and wanted to take care of it."

"Is Sabre doing okay?" DuBois asked.

"Yeah. She's a strong woman. She'll survive this once she stops blaming herself for Harold's death. She knows intellectually it wasn't her fault, but her heart still aches. It'll help once Reggie is convicted. Do you think she'll have to testify?"

"Maybe."

"Will the DA offer him a plea?"

"I think the best they'll do is drop the three older rape charges, but that probably won't be enough for him. We'll just have to wait and see, but I'm certain he'll go away for the murder."

"But the defense will try to discredit Sabre because of her memory loss."

"True enough, but it won't matter. We have insurmountable evidence now. We have his DNA in Sabre's car, on her clothes, and on the rock Harold hit him with. And we have the eyewitness account that corroborates everything. She'll make a good witness. The jury will believe her."

DuBois pulled into the trailer park where the Holloways lived, and JP said, "This is the friend?"

"Yup. She's leaving the old man."

Mrs. Holloway thanked them for coming and invited them inside. Boxes were stacked everywhere, and the walls were stripped, except for a wedding photo of the Holloways.

"I filed for divorce," Mrs. Holloway said. "My son, Faron, is coming to pick me up, and I'm moving to Montana to live with him. I hate to leave Waylon, but he encouraged me to go. In fact, he insisted. I think he's afraid that if Gunner came back for me, I would give in. I'd like to think I wouldn't, but he's probably right. It's better this way."

"Has Gunner been served?" JP asked.

"No, not yet. Faron drove in from Montana last night. He just went to gas up the truck and pick up the trailer. We can start loading as soon as he gets back. After we leave, the sheriff will serve Gunner the papers at his work."

"Where's Porter?"

"He's out of town, but he'll be back tomorrow."

"Does he know you're leaving?"

"No." She shook her head vigorously. "The first thing he would do is run to his daddy and tell him. That's why we're doing this now. I want to be gone before he gets home."

"I'm proud of you," JP said. "I know this isn't easy."

"The hardest part is leaving Waylon, but as soon as he's released, he'll come to live with us in Montana . . . if his probation officer allows it."

"I'm happy for you, and I know that'll make Sabre happy too. She really liked your youngest son in spite of what he did."

Faron showed up, and the three men loaded the truck and trailer under Mrs. Holloway's supervision. It took less than two hours. Mrs. Holloway went inside to check around the house one last time. JP followed her in case she needed some muscle.

"Could you grab that box for me?" she asked.

"Sure."

"That does it, except for one thing." She walked over to the dining room set and stuck a yellow sticky note to the table. She picked up a pen and wrote something on the note. Then she laid something down on the note and walked out without looking back.

JP picked up the box. He stopped at the table on his way out.

DuBois stepped inside just as he did. "What's that?"

"She left her house key with her wedding band attached to the key ring and a note that says nothing but, *Goodbye.*"

"Good for her."

JP and DuBois watched as they pulled away.

DuBois smiled.

"What?" JP asked.

"Nothing."

"You're grinnin' like a possum eatin' a sweet tater."

"Aren't you glad you came?" DuBois asked.

"The only thing better would be to see Gunner's face when he gets served those divorce papers."

Chapter 65

Sabre stopped to check on Angela and then drove down the street and around the corner to Velma Washington's house. Velma had a right to know that Harold was a real hero. She knocked on Velma's door, pleased to find her home.

"It's so nice to see you again, Miss Sabre. Please come in."

"Thank you."

"Come on now. I know you have something important to tell me, so just come in and have a seat. I'll get us some sweet tea. Do you like sweet tea?"

"I don't know if I've ever had it, but if it has caffeine, I can't drink it."

"I have a pitcher already made up without any caffeine."

"Okay, but I don't have a whole lot of time." As soon as Sabre said that, she was sorry. This wonderful old woman did not like to rush, and she really enjoyed her company. "Never mind," Sabre blurted. "You make the tea, and I'll make the time."

Sabre waited in the living room but wandered around, looking at the many photographs of Velma's life. One photo was very old. Sabre tried to figure out if one of the seven little girls in the photo was Velma.

"I'm the one in the middle," Velma said as she returned. She was carrying a glass pitcher of tea on a tray with two large glasses half-filled with ice and a dish of lemon slices. She set the tray on the coffee table and pointed at another photo sitting on her mantle. "That's the last one we had with all of us together."

"Did you have any brothers?"

"No, all girls. I'm sure Papa always wanted a boy, but he never would admit it." She picked up silver tongs and put four slices of lemon in her glass. "It's better if you put the lemon in first. If you want lemon, that is. I find four slices perfect, but you can add more if you'd like."

Sabre followed her lead, and Velma poured the tea into both glasses.

"Do any of your sisters live close by?"

"No." She shook her head. "They're all with Jesus. I don't know why the good Lord spared me, but he did. My youngest sister was the first to go. She was killed in a car accident twenty years ago. My oldest passed away last year, just five days shy of her hundredth birthday. Us girls had a silly bet that started when we were very young. We bet who would live the longest—more specifically, who would make it to a hundred. I guess at the time, we weren't thinking that there would be no way to collect on the bet for whoever was left. But we joked about it over the years."

"Who is in that?" Sabre said, pointing to a black and white photo of a couple.

"Try your tea. I'll tell you all about my family after you tell me about Harold. That's why you're here, isn't it?"

Sabre knew she was stalling, but she couldn't avoid it any longer. "It is," Sabre said. "I got my memory back, all of it." She took a sip of tea and commented on how good it tasted.

"Whatever it is, you can tell me. There isn't much I haven't seen or heard in my ninety-four years. Just spit it out."

Sabre explained what had happened, leaving out a lot of the details, but made a point to tell her what a hero Harold had been. How he had kept her from being raped. How he'd sacrificed his life for hers. "I feel so bad that you lost your friend because of me."

"Heavens to Betsy, child. It sure isn't your fault Harold was killed and don't you blame yourself for one darn minute. If you blame yourself, then you have to blame me, too."

"Why?"

"Because he wouldn't have been here if he wasn't coming to see me," Velma said.

"But he came to the canyon to save me."

"And he came to the area to see me. It's the same argument. And while you're at it, blame the bus company for running the schedule it did, putting him in that spot at that particular moment. And the phone company for not making a phone that charged longer. Otherwise, he would've been able to call someone. And Harold's daddy for not being a better father, or he likely wouldn't have ever moved to California."

Sabre smiled graciously and took another drink of her sweet tea.

"Honey, you can't blame yourself," Velma said. "It's life's circumstances that put Harold where he was. He chose to help you because that's the kind of man he was. I'm so proud that he died a hero. He wanted to make a difference in this world, and he did. Now it's your job to live your life in a way that would make *him* proud. The only one to blame here is the man who killed him. Not you. Not me. Not even the Good Lord for making Harold's father so darn good looking."

This time Sabre smiled from her heart. "You've helped me lift my burden. You're a special lady, Miss Velma Washington."

"So are you, my dear. I can tell you have a good heart."

"Would you mind if I stopped by from time to time? I know I won't be as handy as Harold, but I can be helpful."

"Or you can just stop in for some sweet tea and company."

From the Author

Dear Reader,

Thank you for reading my book. I hope you enjoyed reading it as much as I did writing it. Would you like a FREE copy of a novella about JP when he was young? If so, scan the QR code below and it will take you where you want to go. Or, if you prefer, please go to www.teresaburrell.com and sign up for my mailing list. You'll automatically receive a code to retrieve the story.

SCAN ME

Teresa

Printed in Great Britain
by Amazon

47883090R00152